Loved BY A *Dangerous* DUKE

SEDUCTIVE SCOUNDRELS

COLLETTE CAMERON

Blue Rose Romance®
Portland, Oregon

Sweet-to-Spicy Timeless Romance®

LOVED BY A DANGEROUS DUKE
Seductive Scoundrels
Copyright © 2021 Collette Cameron®
Cover Art: Kim Killion

Attn: Permissions Coordinator
Blue Rose Romance®
8420 N Ivanhoe # 83054
Portland, Oregon 97203

Print Book ISBN: 9781955259026

collettecameron.com

"Aye, I'd give you the moon and stars

if you asked for them."

~Stanford, Duke of Asherford

Other Collette Cameron Books

Seductive Scoundrels

A Diamond for a Duke

Only a Duke Would Dare

A December with a Duke

What Would a Duke Do?

Wooed by a Wicked Duke

Duchess of His Heart

Never Dance with a Duke

Earl of Wainthorpe

Earl of Scarborough

Wedding her Christmas Duke

The Debutante and the Duke

Earl of Keyworth

Loved by a Dangerous Duke

How to Win A Duke's Heart – *Coming soon!*

When a Duke Desires a Lass – *Coming soon!*

Check out Collette's Other Series

Daughters of Desire (Scandalous Ladies)

Highland Heather Romancing a Scot

The Blue Rose Regency Romances:
The Culpepper Misses

Castle Brides

The Honorable Rogues®

Heart of a Scot

Collections

Lords in Love

The Honorable Rogues® Books 1-3

The Honorable Rogues® Books 4-6

Seductive Scoundrels Series Books 1-3

Seductive Scoundrels Series Books 4-6

The Blue Rose Regency Romances:
The Culpepper Misses Series 1-2

Dedication

To everyone who reads in bed
and dreams of chivalrous heroes.

Bedford Square, London

Gravenstones' Ball

17 June 1810

One rotted, moody duke should not be permitted to ruin such a much-anticipated event as the Gravenstones' annual masked ball. Especially as Ophelia had commissioned the cleverest of costumes. She'd never seen anything quite like her ensemble before and was rather proud of her ingenuity.

Festooned in shimmering black and swathed in jet and silver beads and sequins, she'd come as midnight: mysterious, mystical, and exotic. She hoped. Except, she'd spent the better part of an hour hiding from *him*.

Stanford Bancroft, Duke of Asherford, the most deplorable, insulting, arrogant, cold-blooded, mulish peer she'd ever met.

And that was after spending the past three weeks since his proposal peering around corners and skulking around at assemblies, always with the fear of running into him. Why, of late, he'd even intruded upon Ophelia's outings to Hyde Park. She'd taken to glancing behind her or asking one of her friends to enter a room before her all because of his unwanted interest.

Ouch!

"I beg your pardon, Miss Breckensole," Neville Hornbrook mumbled as he missed another step and trod upon her protesting toes. Again.

Sweet Jesus on Sunday.

Despite her throbbing foot, Ophelia fashioned what she hoped was a believable smile as he ineptly partnered her through the steps of a minuet. Perspiring profusely, the bashful banker moved his lips as he counted the dance steps with laborious concentration.

No doubt behind his rooster's mask, his forehead scrunched in concentration as well. His flamboyant tail of red, green, yellow, and blue feathers bobbed and thrashed with his stilted movements, reminding Ophelia of an inebriated cockerel.

Remorse quickened in her for forcing the awkward man onto the dance floor.

But, really?

What choice had she?

Accept Asherford's impending request to dance?

Not that she'd given the pompous bounder the opportunity.

Certainly not.

She would've declined, and then propriety dictated she sit out the rest of the dances this evening. By juniper, Ophelia wasn't moldering away, perched on a chair, when she adored dancing simply because the single man she detested in all of the earth had set his sights on her.

What was more, the dull-witted, obstinate codpate wouldn't take no for an answer.

What kind of man continued to press his suit when the woman of interest made it clear she'd rather wed a toad?

A boorish, clod. That was what kind.

Thinking swiftly to avoid cutting the Duke of Asherford—even Ophelia wasn't such a pea goose as to directly insult *The Dangerous Duke*—she'd practically hauled Mr. Hornbrook onto the dance floor. In truth, she *had* towed the stunned chap along.

The poor man possessed two left feet, and she winced anew as he bumped into her dear friend Rayne Wellbrook.

Rayne smiled graciously, and the tips of Mr. Hornbrook's ears took on a purplish hue above his mask. Neville Hornbrook was, if nothing else, an astute man. He knew full well dancing was not his forte.

Le beau monde balls were heaven or hell, depending on whether one was well received, enjoyed dancing and Society, and whether one spent the evening avoiding a particular jackanape. A buffoon who'd unromantically suggested a union between Ophelia and himself at the Wickerfields' soirée three weeks ago.

Suggested was far too gracious to describe what Asherford had done.

His grace had casually announced in the manner of a general accustomed to immediate and unfettered obedience that he'd chosen Ophelia to be his duchess. He'd been as unemotional as if he'd been selecting which food to bite into next and not picking a wife.

Many empty-headed ninnies and husband-hunting misses might have been ecstatic about his uninspiring proposition.

Ophelia wasn't among them.

It wasn't that she was opposed to marriage, per se, but a marriage of convenience?

Not for her, thank you very much.

Such a union was nothing more than a business arrangement for expediency's sake. Impersonal and mercenary. Unlike most women, marriage wasn't the end-all desire for Ophelia. She wanted more out of life, despite the limited opportunities afforded women in 1810.

She dared a swift perusal of the ballroom as the minuet's steps took her in a wide circle.

Her heart gave an unpleasant leap of surprise when her gaze collided with the Duke of Asherford's vivid blue eyes from across the room. All masculine grace and confidence, arms folded, he leaned a muscled shoulder nonchalantly against one of the doorframes leading onto the terrace. Likely to catch a hint of what meager breeze there might be out of doors.

The overcrowded ballroom was stifling. The air reeked of perfume, sweat, and wax from hundreds of beeswax candles. For the first time, Ophelia rued her choice of costume. Her gown was sweltering, and a trickle of sweat meandered down her spine.

Asherford's mouth moved up into a lazy, roguish smile before she finished her rotation, and their eye contact was broken. A few stanzas later, Ophelia gave a silent thanks that the painstaking dance had finally come to an end. Her grateful toes tingled in appreciation as well.

"Thank you, Mr. Hornbrook."

Ophelia curtsied and, declining to look in Asherford's direction, made straight for the ladies' retiring room. Her nerves were taut as bowstrings, and it peeved her that the duke had any effect on her.

I refuse to let him upset me further.

The retiring room boasted a balcony that overlooked the gardens. Since Ophelia couldn't wander the grounds unchaperoned, she intended to cool off on the quaint gallery. She might even remove her gown and run a damp cloth over her skin. Once she'd regained her equanimity, she'd seek out her twin sister Gabriella, the Duchess of Pennington, or one of her many friends in attendance.

Sophronie Slater and Rayne Wellbrook knew why Ophelia was so vexed with the duke, and they would act as buffers should he continue to seek her out this evening. He would not steal her fun tonight. If the duke became too bothersome, she'd ask her brother-in-law, Maxwell Bronson, Duke of Pennington, to intervene on her behalf. Things weren't so dire that she needed Maxwell's intervention yet, however.

Asherford might be troublesome, but he was a gentleman. Ophelia had no concerns for her safety.

As she wended her way swiftly through the milling crowd, she fought the urge to look behind her. Her nape prickled, and a shiver scuttled across her shoulders and down her arms. Positive that the Duke of Asherford watched her progress, she quickened her pace. Above all, Asherford must not catch her alone again as he had at the Wickerfields'.

She'd vow he'd orchestrated that *chance* rendezvous.

Fool me once, shame on you. Fool me twice, shame on me.

Of its own accord, her upper lip tilted up slightly into a sneer before she schooled her mouth into a pleasant line. Ladies did not sneer or scowl. She was well-practiced in tempering tart retorts and painting a benign mien upon her features when turmoil cavorted about inside her head.

Thank goodness no one knew what went on in her mind. They'd be shocked and appalled. Gabriella was the high-spirited, outspoken sister. Ophelia was the well-mannered, docile twin.

Or so everyone mistakenly believed.

Her rancor toward the Duke of Asherford hadn't eased these past weeks. How could it when he continually showed up at events she attended? Much like rubbing salt into a wound, he pursued her with a doggedness that might have been admirable if his attentions weren't so unwelcome.

The duke hadn't even bothered to cushion his insulting proposal with compliments or a degree of finesse. His words rang in her ears just as loudly and offensively as if he'd spoken them but minutes before and not three weeks ago.

"Miss Breckensole, I have decided we should wed. You are of satisfactory lineage, and from my observation of you these past weeks, I have concluded your temperament and decorum are adequate. I require a wife and heir. I am confident we would suit sufficiently."

Satisfactory lineage. Temperament and decorum are adequate. Suit sufficiently.

I require an heir? An heir?

Oh, of all the unmitigated gall.

Her reply had been concise.

"No, Your Grace."

Her comportment had been polite and reserved, revealing nothing of the dervish spinning inside her.

Until he persisted in listing how qualified she was for such an honor.

Dumping her glass of lemonade on his suit had

quite squelched his protestations.

Now waving her black lace fan rapidly to cool her heated face, Ophelia tucked her chin and indulged in a gleeful chuckle as she reached the last riser and turned to the left toward the retiring room.

Her prompt response had taken the starch right out of his ducal self. No doubt *The Dangerous Duke,* as Asherford was called behind his back—none dared speak the moniker to his face—hadn't considered she'd refuse, much less fail to thank him for the privilege.

She hadn't even offered an excuse. Just a firm "No."

Oh, and the lemonade, of course.

Regardless, Ophelia had been silently hurling insults at him in her mind.

None of the *ton* or lower orders denied Stanford Bancroft, Duke of Asherford, anything, as his unflattering nickname alluded to.

"Until now," she muttered to herself.

"Until now, what?"

Mouth parting on a strangled screech, Ophelia jerked her head up. She barely succeeded in stumbling to a stop before plowing straight into the too wide chest of the very man she'd been musing about.

Bother and blast.

Asherford grasped her elbows, steadying her, his touch surprisingly gentle for such a large man—a man known for his emotionlessness and lack of empathy.

Heat zipped up her arms, and she stepped backward, snapping her fan shut. She'd much rather whack him with the accessory for giving her such a start. Even now, her pulse ticked in her throat as frantically as a netted bird beating its wings.

"You may release me. I assure you, I am in no danger of falling, Your Grace."

At once, he released her but not before his mouth twitched in amusement.

His humor raised Ophelia's hackles, and the urge to hit him again rose within her like a wave crashing to the shore.

Why did he have to be the single man who brought out the worst in her?

Usually, she was good-natured, patient, and genial. And assuredly not moved to violence.

How in the blazes had Asherford managed to get upstairs before her anyway? What was more, how had he known she'd seek the retiring room and not return to her friends or family after the dance?

"I knew you'd retreat," he said dryly as if reading her mind.

Ophelia did not like that in the least. That he anticipated her actions unnerved her in a manner she couldn't describe. Tilting her head to meet his piercing blue eyes rimmed in violet peering at her from behind his peacock feather mask, she straightened her spine.

Must he be so dashed tall?

He stood at least a head above every other man she knew. Even when she wasn't looking for him, he was easily spotted because of his height and hair so raven black, it looked blue in some light.

"You err. I am not running away, Your Grace."

Ophelia *was* fleeing in a manner of speaking. Nonetheless, she would gargle nails before admitting anything of the sort to *him*. Instead, she raised what she hoped was an imperious eyebrow, then she realized her mask hid her calculated move.

Just as well. Ophelia was utter rot at such machinations.

"I am merely overly warm and wish to apply a damp towel to my face." Assuredly, she wasn't going to mention the other activities that took place in the ladies' retiring room.

"I have just the solution then," Asherford offered with a smile that was designed to melt iron.

Ophelia was well on her way to wilting from the heat already.

"Your costume is quite extraordinary and most becoming." His voice dipped a seductive octave. "But I'm afraid I'm at a loss to know what you represent."

"I'm midnight." How she wished it was midnight, and she might excuse herself for supper.

"Ah. Yes, I see it now. Brilliant." He raked his appreciative gaze over her.

Despite her dislike of the man, Ophelia couldn't prevent the swell of feminine pride that sent another wave of heat over her body. She snapped her fan open and waved it energetically.

"There's a small widow's walk accessible through

the turret," he said.

How did he know that?

Did Asherford make a point of prowling about peoples' houses without their knowledge?

"The Gravenstones are cousins of mine on my mother's side," he offered in explanation as if reading her thoughts once more. "I know the house well."

Well, that explained that.

"The breeze will be unobstructed at that height," he said unnecessarily.

Asherford tipped his firm mouth into an inviting smile and extended his elbow. Several of the dukes had coordinated their costumes and dressed as peacocks. His purple cloak shimmered and sparkled as if it had a life of its own. The sequins adorning the garment made it appear as if the color changed with his movements.

Ophelia refused to acknowledge how the purple of his cloak made his eyes appear nearly lavender. Men should not have pretty eyes—particularly men with a reputation for being merciless and without a sense of humor.

"No, thank you. Please excuse me." She made to

move around him, and he politely stepped to the side.

"You will say yes, one day, Ophelia."

The timbre of his voice caused another shiver to scamper from her waist, up her spine, and spread over her shoulders like a woolen mantle.

Halting, she glanced behind her. "Don't be so sure of that, Your Grace. Even *you* cannot always have your way."

He didn't even try to hide his superior grin. He flashed his straight white teeth and chuckled low and dangerous.

"I *always* have my way, Ophelia. Always."

Unnerving conviction echoed in the Duke of Asherford's tenor.

"Not this time." Ophelia glared at him, past caring about politesse. Perhaps if she acted the shrew, he'd leave off pursuing her. "Look elsewhere for a bride. I'm not interested, nor will I ever be."

To be married to such a domineering man would smother her. Her heart beating a syncopated staccato, Ophelia proceeded toward the retiring room at a measured pace.

You're running away.

Yes, yes, she was.

There was a time to confront the enemy.

This was not it. Prudence was the better part of valor.

"We shall see, my frightened little rabbit."

Ophelia gritted her teeth as she gripped the door handle. "Indeed, we shall," she muttered to herself. "I shall not be manipulated into a marriage I do not want."

Stanford knew when to make a strategic exit. He'd only attended tonight in this ridiculous peacock travesty because it meant another opportunity to speak with Ophelia Breckensole about a match between them.

He wasn't quite ready to approach the Duke of Pennington, her brother-in-law, to ask for her hand. There was also a grandfather in Colchester who must be spoken with as well. But Stan, as he was known to his closest friends, preferred Ophelia, a willing participant.

After all, they faced decades together. Far better a cordial relationship than an apathetic or hostile one.

Besides, she was of age, and at one and twenty, it really wasn't for anyone else to say who she should wed.

Stan wasn't such an ogre that he'd force her into marriage.

It simply had never occurred to him that she'd refuse his suit. Women tripped over themselves to be in his company, and Stan damn well knew his company was not pleasant.

His initial approach to Ophelia had been faulty. He realized that now.

Ophelia Breckensole was the type of woman who needed to be wooed. His finely honed instincts told him traditional courtship would get him nowhere. The problem was that he knew nothing about such frivolities. Before this, he'd considered courtship a waste of time and money. And a man of his position was hardly going to ask for assistance.

From the moment he'd first seen Ophelia Breckensole at Westfall's ball last April, Stan had known there was something different about her than the other debutantes and marriage-minded misses. There was an aura about Ophelia, a freshness and vivacity the others lacked.

Something about her beckoned him, made him want to make her his own. From her clear hazel eyes, alight with keen intelligence and a bit of mischief, to her hair, a conglomeration of brown and blond tones, to her contagious smile—she'd enthralled him.

It might be because she'd been raised in the country and lacked the artifice so many women of noble birth affected. In any event, of all the women he'd met in his nine and twenty years, she stirred something in him more than lust. Desire might fade in time, and it was imperative he could tolerate his wife across the breakfast table every morning. A woman who could carry on an intelligent conversation and was pleasantly tempered was a bonus.

And so Stan had determined she should be his duchess.

It wasn't a rash, impulsive urge but rather a calculated, rational decision based on compatibility.

Although he hadn't intended to wed just yet, Stan had never doubted he'd take a wife.

Unlike the prior lackadaisical Dukes of Asherford, he took his responsibilities to the dukedom seriously. Far too seriously, many accused. Generally, those he'd refused to forgive a debt owed. He wasn't known for his benevolence nor his compassion, but he was logical and fair-minded.

Had those charging him with a mercenary character inherited failing estates and massive debts at fourteen, perhaps they'd be a trifle somber and austere too. He hadn't even gone to university but had spent nearly every waking hour since his sire's death working toward one goal: making the Asherford dukedom the envy of the peerage, rather than the object of pity and contempt.

He'd succeeded by the time he was five and twenty. Now it was time to do his duty and sire an heir. Three sons ought to secure the dukedom's future nicely.

A memory of Ophelia's flashing hazel eyes glaring up at him, her creamy skin bearing a hint of rose across her defined cheeks as she refused his marriage offer, made him grin.

She'd settled those lush pink lips into a pleasant—rehearsed, he'd wager—curve and flat out declined him. And then, in an unexpected display of impoliteness, deposited her lemonade on his coat.

Ophelia wasn't, by nature, cantankerous, spoiled, or demanding. He'd not have selected her to be his bride if she had been. The lemonade she'd dumped on his suit in response to his less than cavalier insistence that she met the qualifications to become his duchess was deserved.

Well-deserved, in truth.

He'd been a pompous arse.

Stan had no objection to a woman with spirit, as long as she knew how to control herself. Ophelia Breckensole would be his and willingly too. He just had to convince her that was what she wanted.

Ignoring those attempting to catch his eye as he made his way to the entry, Stan considered his next move in his courtship of Ophelia. Not flowers or sweets. Something more meaningful.

"Asherford, you're just the man to settle a matter."

Pausing, Stan produced a rare but genuine smile of pleasure. "Sutcliffe. You're looking well. Marriage agrees with you, it seems."

Several of Stan's friends had wed in the past year, and all appeared happy as grigs. But then again, theirs had been love matches. He supposed that was well and good for them, but he'd lived the past fifteen years on his wit, intellect, and keen ability to read people and situations. He wasn't going to muck up his well-ordered life with sentimental entanglements.

Victor, Duke of Sutcliffe, grinned in return. "Indeed, it does."

He inclined his head toward his three ducal companions.

Stan acknowledged the trio, all of whom were also members of *Bon Chance*, along with himself and Sutcliffe, with a slight canting of his head.

"Sheffield, Waycross, Heatherston, and I are at an impasse. Sheffield and I believe gas for lighting will become commonplace. Gas lights in every home. We think it is an industry that would garner significant profits and is worth investing in. However, Waycross and Heatherston are convinced only the wealthy will take to gas lighting. What say you?"

Waycross and Heatherston were Scots, and they had a valid point. But so did Sutcliffe and Sheffield. Though why they thought the matter so significant that it required discussion at a masked ball was beyond Stan.

"I do see a future in gas lighting," he agreed. "Nonetheless, I don't believe the masses will embrace the concept for decades. They cannot afford to."

The dukes of Waycross and Heatherston exchanged satisfied glances. Unfortunately, gas for lighting was far less likely to become common in the Highlands for even longer.

"Were I you," Stan looked to each of them in turn, "I'd be investing in Durand's tin can and that German fellow's new printing press. And steam engines." He gave a sage nod for emphasis. "Mark my word. Engines are the way of the future. I shan't be surprised if there are horseless carriages someday. The world is changing, and we must change with it."

Sheffield scratched his jaw. "Interesting and rather fascinating."

"Aye, but I dinna like some of the changes." Waycross shook his head as he gazed across the room. "A woman should ken her place."

That sentiment was also changing, thanks to innovators like Mary Wollstonecraft. Nevertheless, Stan wasn't in the mood to upend that bucket of worms.

Above the other men's heads, he caught sight of Ophelia reentering the ballroom, looking much refreshed. She was met at once by several women, including the American giving Waycross fits, Sophronie Slater, and Justina Farthington.

Miss Slater looped her hand through Ophelia's arm and began leading her toward a small crowd clustered at one end of the ballroom.

Ophelia glanced over her shoulder. Her lovely eyes rounded when she spied Stan, and a blush stained her cheeks before she averted her gaze and presented her profile.

If Stan were the type of man to take affront or to feel chagrin, he might flush himself. But as he was a pragmatic sort, he simply filed her response away to examine later.

"Ah, so that's the way the wind blows, is it?" Sutcliffe asked, his voice ringing with hilarity. "I know Ophelia Breckensole well. You better have a well-thought-out strategy, Asherford. She's not as biddable as she presents."

Bollocks.

"I'm sure I don't know what you mean," Stan said stiffly, feeling as awkward as a lad caught pilfering a ginger biscuit.

"I'm sure you don't." Sheffield chuckled. "But you will, my friend. My sympathies."

He slapped Stan on the shoulder.

Why did blissfully married men think they were experts on courtship?

A scowl lashed Waycross's eyebrows together as he watched Ophelia and Miss Slater's progress across the room. It was well-known that the American had acquired a mare Waycross had been waiting to purchase for breeding purposes. He hadn't forgiven her for her temerity or for buying the mare out from under him.

"I heard the gypsies have camped on Gipsy Hill and have set up a fair of sorts. They have horseflesh for sale. If I can get there before that she-devil does," Waycross said.

"Aye." Heatherston nodded. "I have a mind to take a gander myself."

"I shan't be surprised if half of the *ton* isn't there tomorrow afternoon to have their fortunes told and pick up a knick-knack or two." Sheffield flicked a speck of something off the front of his cape. "I've promised to accompany my wife. I believe several of her friends are also intent on an outing to the gypsy encampment, including the Duchess of Pennington."

That was as subtle as the portly Prince Regent prancing about in pink satin.

Regardless, Stan appreciated the hint. It meant Ophelia would likely accompany her twin. Gratitude wasn't a sentiment he expressed with ease, but he gave Sheffield a terse nod of affirmation.

Stan hadn't planned on wasting time meandering about the travellers' camp, and he had no interest in having his fortune read. He didn't believe in that preternatural poppycock.

The travellers came through annually, and every year, London went slightly berserk at their appearance. The Roma stopped in the wooded area of Gipsy Hill near Croydon, where a few made the place their permanent home.

London's elite were fascinated by the travellers— more so by the prospect of learning their futures from one of the fortunetellers.

Stan had never been particularly interested in the

nomads' simple life, culture, and mysticism that *le beau monde* found so intriguing. Nevertheless, if Ophelia was going to Gipsy Hill tomorrow, it might prove a perfect opportunity to learn more about her. Such knowledge could only aid in his quest to make her his wife.

"Perhaps I'll see you there," he said with a noncommittal nod. "Please excuse me."

The others bid him farewell and wandered away, soon disappearing into the throng.

Stan asked a footman to call for his coach. Shortly thereafter, he sat within, pondering his next move. Was it because Ophelia Breckensole presented a challenge that Stan pursued her?

"Not this time. Look elsewhere for a bride. I'm not interested, nor will I ever be."

Since he'd been fourteen, when he'd set his mind to a task, he didn't give up until he succeeded. And of all of the obstacles he'd faced, convincing Ophelia to be his duchess might be the greatest. He saw now that he'd gone about it all wrong. She'd have to be won. That meant he'd have to cast off his protective shroud. A guise he'd adopted as a scared, uncertain fourteen-year-old to fend off his own and others' doubts.

The Dangerous Duke could not win Ophelia Breckensole's hand in marriage.

Could Stanford Bancroft?

3

Gypsy Encampment

Gipsy Hill

The next afternoon

Ophelia clapped her hands in time as two talented fiddlers zipped their bows across the instruments' strings with skill and speed she'd never before witnessed. A trio of pixy-faced children danced and performed acrobatics for the crowd's amusement. Ebony-haired and with eyes such a deep coffee brown they looked almost black, the children wore colorful clothing and grinned nonstop.

The front teeth of the youngest, not more than six, were missing. He kept sticking the tip of his tongue through the gap when he performed a challenging movement.

This was Ophelia's first venture to Gipsy Hill, and she adored everything about the outing so far. She'd already purchased two baskets, a scarf, and a carved box. And she'd only been here a quarter hour.

Roma, commoners, and London's elite roamed the good-sized encampment as if there wasn't a vast difference in their stations. Here and there, clusters of gypsy women chatted as they wove baskets or worked at other tasks. Several men surrounded a makeshift wrestling ring and called encouragement to the opponent they favored.

Ophelia examined the fair, trying to decide where she'd most like to go next. There was so much to see. It was hard to choose.

Her gaze collided with a bare-chested, neatly bearded young man with shoulder-length hair. He must've just finished a wrestling match. Wiping sweat from his torso with a cloth, he boldly assessed her. A slow grin bowed his mouth. Clasping a brown arm across his waist, he bent into an exaggerated bow.

His companions, seeing his preoccupation, turned to look where their friend stared.

Oddly unnerved, Ophelia dropped her gaze at once.

Likely, her discomfiture stemmed from seeing half-clothed gypsies and their casual indifference about their state of undress. Only one other man had dared to stare at her so boldly.

The Duke of Asherford.

At once, she quashed thoughts of him.

Today was meant to be a pleasant diversion.

The afternoon was warm, but an agreeable breeze and the shade from the copse of trees the travellers had camped beneath kept the temperature reasonable. Maxwell had delivered hers and Gabriella's treasures to the carriage and was now striding in their direction.

More than one woman turned to look after him, but he only had eyes for his duchess. Ophelia had thought him the worst sort of ogre when he'd first approached Gabriella about marriage. He'd proved himself by his unwavering devotion to Ophelia's twin.

Maxwell was the brother she'd never had, and she'd come to love him as such.

Gabriella and Maxwell's situation was much different than what Asherford had proposed to Ophelia, however. Maxwell's motive for making Gabriella his wife had been revenge, which had turned into a deep and abiding love.

At least Maxwell had been passionate about his desire to make Gabriella his wife, if for the wrong reason. Asherford addressed marriage with the same enthusiasm and emotion as one chose a piece of toast for breakfast.

"I think I shall get my fortune read," Gabriella said, twirling her silk parasol. The pink fringe edging the accessory fluttered with the movement. "Would you like to join me?"

She included Sophronie and Ophelia in her invitation.

"No, thank you, Gabriella. I still haven't seen the horses." Unabashed, Sophronie grinned, and her slightly crooked front tooth didn't detract from her prettiness. Blue eyes alight with mischief, she seized Ophelia's hand. "Come with me. I cannot go by myself."

No lady could walk about the camp unescorted.

"Ronie, you'd sleep with horses if it was permissible." Ophelia laughed. Never had she met a woman more obsessed with horseflesh than this American.

"I did in America. Several times, in fact," Sophronie said proudly.

"Should I be shocked?" Ophelia muttered drolly, not shocked in the least.

Gabriella's and Sophronie's laughter melded with hers.

Fishing in her reticule for a few coins, Ophelia tossed them in the violin case set before the dancing children as she'd seen several others watching the performance do.

"I'll go with Ronie, Gabby."

"Be careful, Fee Fee," her sister said, using the pet name she'd called her since they'd learned to talk. "I'm sure it's quite safe, but it never hurts to be aware. Stay together."

Gabriella wasn't one to worry without cause. Ophelia glanced toward the wrestling ring, but the man who'd made her uncomfortable was gone.

"Where are you two off to?" Gabriella's husband asked when he reached them.

"To look at the horses, Your Grace," Sophronie put in. "I might see an animal or two I simply must add to our stables back home."

Personally, Ophelia didn't think the horses would enjoy the voyage.

Sophronie and her father bred thoroughbreds in the United States. They were creating quite a name for themselves in racing circles in both Britain and America.

Grinning, Maxwell shook his head before taking his wife's elbow. "Why am I not surprised?"

Sophronie shrugged, seeming to not care in the least that her fascination with horseflesh wasn't *de rigor* amongst the *ton*.

In truth, Ophelia would prefer to explore the encampment than have her fortune told. In that way, she was different than her twin. Preternatural dabblings had always given her the heebie-jeebies, even if it was claptrap and rot.

"Come along, Ophelia." Sophronie tugged at Ophelia's hand. "I see that bounder Waycross heading toward the corral."

Corral was a generous description of the roped-off area.

Ophelia looked to where her frowning friend stared and bit back an unladylike oath. Waycross wasn't alone. The Duke of Asherford strode beside him, though the men's backs were to the women, so he hadn't spied her yet.

"I always have my way, Ophelia. Always."

She shuddered anew upon recalling his husky whisper.

Having her palm read didn't seem so disagreeable after all.

"Must we look at the horses just now?" After last night, Ophelia wasn't at all kindly disposed to spend time in the company of the duke.

Sophronie gave a toss of her head, causing the loose strawberry blond curls piled atop her head to jiggle.

"And let that Highland boor have the first pick? I think not. The Duke of Waycross has been intolerable since I outbid him at Tattersalls. He acts as if it were a personal affront, for pity's sake. It was business, not a slur upon his character. I wanted the mare for our stables, plain and simple. I outbid him. If he wanted her, he ought to have bid higher. He's behaving like a spoiled child."

Maxwell had mentioned that many people believed Waycross to be miserly and stingy, but the truth of it was, he wasn't flush in the pockets. So he'd ventured into horse breeding a few years ago as a means of restoring his family's financial standing.

Ophelia almost pitied the man. Except he'd been unpardonably rude to Sophronie.

"Do hurry, Ophelia," her friend urged, making no effort to disguise her impatience.

Ophelia suspected Sophronie enjoyed the verbal sparring with Waycross, though she'd walk on hot coals before admitting it.

Like you do with Asherford?

I do not!

Don't you?

Of all the ridiculous notions. Now Ophelia's mood

had turned quite sour.

Puffing her cheeks out into a silent, almost childish sigh, she grudgingly conceded. Neither she nor Sophronie should be wandering the encampment alone. "After the horses, I want to look at those hand-painted fans across the way. And try those pastries. They smell heavenly."

"Of course," Sophronie agreed, tugging Ophelia across the hard ground with an alacrity that belied her petite form. She'd have agreed to anything if it meant spending time with equines.

"Oh my stars, look at him," Sophronie breathed. Eyes round, she moved trancelike toward a glistening ebony Friesian. "He's magnificent. A perfect specimen."

Yes, he is.

"Just look at that glorious mane."

What? Mane?

Ophelia blinked as heat burned dual paths up her cheeks.

Nincompoop.

Her friend spoke of the horse they approached and

not the Duke of Asherford as he murmured softly to a dove gray mare and rubbed her forehead. She pressed her head into him, welcoming his caress.

Sophronie released Ophelia and approached the horse.

"He's *mine,* lass," came a distinctly frosty Scottish burr.

Giving Asherford her back, not that he knew she was there, Ophelia regarded the tableau before her. Tension fairly sparked in the air, as if a bolt of lightning might shoot from the heavens and strike the ground where they stood.

The Roma holding the horse's halter swung his dark-eyed gaze from Sophronie to the Duke of Waycross. Ah, the perceptive traveller had detected Sophronie's keen interest and seized the opportunity as any shrewd hawker would.

The Friesian nickered softly when Sophronie ran a practiced hand along his wither. She cut the gypsy a sideways look. "Is he sold?"

"Aye," came Waycross's instant, clipped reply. "To me. Yer too late this time."

"Not yet," the Roma said with an apologetic shrug and grin toward the duke. "Let's discuss this noble creature, shall we?"

"Nae," Waycross all but growled. "I saw him first."

"Fiddle faddle." Waving her hand, Sophronie swept her mouth into a falsely bright smile. "Good sir," she said to the gypsy, "I do believe a thorough discussion is in order."

"Shall we leave them to their argument?" A masculine voice rumbled near Ophelia's ear.

How had Asherford approached so silently?

She'd hadn't been that engrossed with the quarrel playing out before her.

"It may take some time," he mused. "Waycross is still livid that Miss Slater outbid him at Tattersalls. He shan't give that magnificent beast up without a fight."

He was right.

God only knew how long she might stand here eavesdropping on their squabble. The Duke of Waycross could escort Sophronie back to Gabriella and Maxwell. Being forced to bear one another's company for propriety's sake served the two of them right for always quarreling.

"I don't know how long Maxwell and Gabriella plan on staying, and there are several other things I should like to see before we leave." Ophelia wrinkled her nose, her attention migrating from Sophronie and the Scotsman. "Are you certain we should leave them alone together?"

"Indeed. They need to have this out." Black eyebrow cocked rakishly, Asherford presented his elbow. Humor had softened the harsh contours of his face. "Permit me to accompany you, Miss Breckensole." He caught the Duke of Waycross's eye. "Waycross, I leave Miss Slater in your care."

"What? No," came Miss Slater's immediate, horrified reply. "You cannot."

"Nae, I want nothin' to do with the banshee," Waycross objected with a ferocious scowl toward Sophronie.

"Pretend you don't hear them, Ophelia," Asherford whispered, steering her away. "Waycross is too much of a gentleman to desert her, even if he can't stand Miss Slater. She'll be fine. I promise."

Ophelia slid her hand into the bend of his arm, doing her utmost not to notice his deliciously firm muscles. Or that he smelled rather pleasantly of a woodsy cologne.

Cedar? Pine? Eucalyptus?

Without stepping nearer and sniffing deeply, she couldn't be certain.

Casting a glance over her shoulder, Ophelia relaxed. Both Sophronie and Waycross had turned their backs and were immersed in a deep discussion with the horse handler. He'd tied off the Friesian and brought over two more impressive horses.

"Where to Miss Breckensole?" Asherford asked as if she were the queen, and he was her devoted courtier. This Duke of Asherford was almost likable.

"Over there." She tilted her head in the direction of a display with fans and crocheted gloves.

As they maneuvered their way through the curiosity seekers and laden tables and barrel tops, he asked, "Are you enjoying yourself?"

Ophelia looked at him archly.

Since when did *he* indulge in small talk?

Tranquil blue eyes gazed back at her. Typically, Asherford's eyes were turbulent and penetrating. This calm, engaging man set her nerves on edge worse than the pompous one. At least she knew what to expect from that duke.

"I am," Ophelia admitted after a moment. "I admire the travellers for their industriousness and their traditions. Theirs is not an easy life, but look how happy they are? I vow, they wear perpetual smiles."

"Happiness comes from within, pretty lady," a gypsy said in the creaky, papery voice of the elderly.

Ophelia smiled at the woman sitting on a three-legged stool before a colorful, beautifully decorated, and engraved vardo.

The gypsy unfurled a gnarled hand and gestured toward two other painted stools. "Sit. Vadoma will tell you your futures. Vadoma is never wrong. I am a true *drabarni*—fortuneteller. I don't whisper *darane svatura*—superstitious stories. *I* hear from God."

She seemed so confident that Ophelia almost believed her.

"No—"

She was about to politely decline when the Duke of Asherford flummoxed her by grinning and pulling her to sit on one of the short stools. He balanced his tall frame on the other, his eyes glinting with devilish humor.

"Good. Good," Vadoma said before taking a puff on her pipe. Closing her eyes, she hummed softly to herself as she gently swayed, inhaling from her pipe every now and again.

Ophelia cast Stanford a questioning glance.

Didn't the gypsy need to examine their palms? Or at least pretend trancelike mysticism while staring into a glass ball and muttering weird incantations?

Grinning wider, almost boyishly and carefree, Stanford lifted a shoulder in an I-don't-know-either shrug.

Ophelia should not have noticed how the movement caused the rich navy-blue fabric to pull taut over his sculpted muscles. Having never seen him anything other than staid and somber, she had no idea what to make of this charming version of the Duke of Asherford. Why, in truth, he was quite handsome when he wasn't scowling darkly.

Vadoma opened her black eyes and smiled. The movement crumpled her already deeply lined face into deep pleats like a folded fan. She pulled the pipe from her mouth and rested it on her knee. Then, peering directly at the duke, she leaned forward. Her unyielding gaze trained upon him, she pointed a boney finger.

"What you desire is not yours to take. It must be given freely."

She slowly veered her black-eyed gaze to Ophelia, staring keenly.

Ophelia resisted the urge to squirm on the stool.

Vadoma puffed on her pipe twice. "You will help him make the right choice."

Struck dumb by the declaration, Ophelia simply stared, jaw slack, at the woman.

Help him?

Extending her palm, Vadoma waited for her payment.

Asherford obliged her and most generously too.

Curling her fingers around the coins, Vadoma returned her pipe to her mouth. She rose and climbed the four narrow steps to her wagon with the stiff movements of the aged. At the top, she paused and scanned her uncanny, probing gaze over Ophelia and then the duke.

A nascent smile pulling at her mouth, Vadoma's eyes softened, and a faraway look entered them. Speaking around her pipe stem, she said, "As the Romani proverbs say, 'We are all wanderers on this earth. Our hearts are full of wonder, and our souls are deep with dreams.' Be careful that your dreams do not destroy another's."

Before Ophelia could ask her to clarify, the bright yellow door snicked shut behind the old woman.

Had Vadoma meant those last words for Ophelia or for the duke?

4

That had definitely been an irregular experience. Eerie too.

Vadoma spoke with such conviction and authority. It was difficult to dismiss her prophecy as mystical twaddle. Though Stan didn't hold with such fustian rubbish as fortune telling and palm reading, the old gypsy's words kept running through his mind.

"What you desire is not yours to take. It must be given freely." And *"Be careful that your dreams do not destroy another's."*

He'd been watching Ophelia and had seen the color leech from her face. The gypsy's words had disconcerted her. As always, however, she recovered quickly and, in a thrice, had smoothed her expression into polite indifference.

"Shall we find my sister?" Ophelia asked as she stood and gazed around the bustling encampment.

Across the way, a man juggled four wicked-looking knives before a rapt audience.

A delicious aroma wafted past, and Stan's stomach growled in appreciation.

He'd skipped breakfast for an early morning meeting and forgone lunch to finish his work for the day so that he could join the other privileged citizens touring the travellers' encampment today.

Ophelia raised her dainty nose and sniffed. "My goodness. Something smells scrumptious." She half-turned and sniffed again. "There. Where that group of people is watching that woman fry something." She gave him a mischievous grin. "I'm starving. I rushed my breakfast."

Few ladies admitted to a hearty appetite. Instead, most picked at their food when eating in public.

Stan chuckled as he fell into place beside her. "I'm rather hungry myself."

In short order, they both held a warm flatbread.

Grinning with pride, the Romani woman encouraged them to take a bite. "It is called manriklo," she said in a melodic contralto. "Eat. Eat."

She gestured to her mouth with her fingertips.

Stan dutifully took a bite at the same time Ophelia did.

Her eyes rounded in delight, and she took a bigger bite.

"Umm, it's amazing." She closed her eyes just before she flicked her tongue out to catch a crumb on the plump pillow of her lower lip. "Mmm," she practically moaned.

Stan gritted his teeth against the rush of desire that flooded his groin at her innocent actions.

He shoved half the bread into his mouth, nearly choking himself. As he'd hoped, his carnal urges evaporated. After all, breathing was more important than lusting after a beautiful woman.

Wasn't it?

The savory toasted circle contained herbs and cheese, and Stan finished his in three bites. He paid for two more.

"Thank you," he said to the gypsy, who had already turned her attention to the next customer.

Balancing the warm bread on his handkerchief, he took Ophelia's elbow.

Chewing, she gave him a side-eyed glance but didn't object as he led her to a stand of trees near the camp's perimeter. It was quieter here, providing an ideal backdrop to finish their snack and still observe the many fascinating performers. And as they were in full view of everyone, he needn't worry about unsavory conjectures.

Or perhaps, to be more accurate, no more than the usual speculative *on dit* that inevitably surrounded an unmarried duke.

An angry bird scolded them from overhead. Stan tipped his head upward but couldn't spy the outraged creature amongst the oaks' branches. Or the other nearby trees, either. Perhaps it was farther back in the thicker woods behind them.

Ophelia finished her bread and wiped her mouth with a lacy scrap of cloth. "That was utterly fabulous."

"Here." Stan offered her another. "Be careful. It's still quite warm."

Giving him a cheeky grin, she accepted the manriklo and leaned her slender back against an oak. "I won't have any appetite for dinner, but these are simply too delectable. I wonder if Maxwell's cook might be persuaded to make them?" She eyed the one in her hand. "I'd like to try one with marmalade or raspberry preserves, but perhaps without the herbs and cheese."

Bracing one foot on a raised root, Stan leaned a shoulder against the same tree, far nearer to Ophelia than was proper. So much for not stirring gossip.

Stan couldn't bring himself to care two damns.

Ophelia hadn't bristled and become all prickly like she usually did in his presence. Was the way to her heart as simple as feeding her? If so, tomorrow, Stan would send her chocolates and sweetmeats. Or candied almonds, marzipan, and Cook's most excellent lemon curd.

Finishing his second manriklo, he studied Ophelia's face. Her pale green and light blue ensemble complimented her hazel eyes and ivory skin. She radiated contentment and joy. This was the most relaxed she'd ever been around him.

"This is nice." Giving a satisfied sigh, Ophelia tucked her hands behind her back and curved her full mouth upward. A breeze flirted with the ends of her bonnet's sky-blue ribbons and a honey-colored curl near her ear.

"I like it when you smile, Ophelia."

She looked up at him through her thick lashes.

Not in a coquettish manner, but with genuine consideration.

"I do so much of the time, Your Grace."

"Not at me."

A flicker of something undefinable flashed within her eyes, and Ophelia turned her gaze away. "It's not intentional, Your Grace."

The magic of the moment vanished, blown away like thistledown in a gale.

Stan inwardly cursed himself for being a thousand kinds of a fool. He and Ophelia had been getting on famously, and then he had to ruin the moment by making it too personal. She'd taken offense at his remark. The Dangerous Duke might've continued along the previous track, but Stanford Bancroft was a more sensitive man.

"I know it's not, Ophelia."

Stan's tongue was dry from the two flatbreads. Or was it from sticking his entire foot in his mouth?

"I'll get us something to drink," he said, keeping his tone deliberately light and casual.

"I would be grateful." Ophelia's eyes lit with appreciation. In the trees' shade, they appeared more blue than hazel.

Today she wasn't holding a grudge, it seemed.

Pushing away from the oak's trunk, Ophelia brushed a few crumbs from her spencer. After stepping over a gnarled root that twisted across the ground, she wandered to the other side of the large tree. Actually, two oaks had grown together, creating a massive tree about six feet wide that separated about twelve feet up.

From overhead, the perturbed bird insistently called an alarm.

Placing a hand over her eyes, Ophelia peered upward.

Stan searched the area nearby for a drink of some sort.

A pair of young women were ladling an amber liquid into mugs about forty feet away. The beverage was popular. The women couldn't keep up with the demand, mostly from young bucks and Roma men.

"I'll be just a minute, Ophelia," Stan said. "Don't wander too far."

He could see her from the clearing, and no one else had sought refuge under that particular stand. It wasn't as if she were alone with all of these people wandering about anyway. Still, it wouldn't do to tempt fate.

"I won't." She gave a little waggle of her fingers and continued to search the upper branches. "I hear you," she murmured. "Where are you? What kind of bird are you? A noisy one, but then your home has been invaded, hasn't it? I'm sorry. The Roma will leave in a few weeks, and you'll have your quiet home back."

Grinning at her inane conversation with an invisible bird, Stan strode the few feet to the beverage stand. The women were serving a frothy ale. No wonder the brew was so popular. Shifting his feet impatiently, he waited his turn, and after tipping the gypsies and promising to return the mugs, he pivoted to return to Ophelia.

Where was she?

Her blue and green gown shouldn't blend in with the trunks and shadows. Unfortunately, she was no longer visible through the trees.

Quickening his stride, he hurried forward, the ale sloshing onto his hands in his haste.

Entering the trees' cool shade, he called her name. "Ophelia?"

The blasted bird screamed louder. Only, it wasn't a bird at all, but an outraged squirrel sitting on a branch and twitching its bushy tail. Its tiny black eyes were riveted on something in the distance.

Ophelia?

Bloody, bloody hell.

And she wasn't alone. A muscular gypsy had a hand over her mouth and was dragging her, struggling and thrashing, farther into the woodlands.

Her wide, terrified gaze sought Stan's.

"Help me." She silently pleaded.

5

Ophelia writhed and twisted, trying to kick her assailant in the shins or ankle. She struggled to breathe against the bruising palm clamped over her mouth. Terror sluiced through her veins, one second causing her to tremble from clammy chills and the next infusing her with scorching heat.

"Stop fighting, English witch," her attacker growled into her ear, the timbre of his voice the lyrical accent of the travellers.

The man had come upon her unawares.

Stupid, stupid girl.

Engrossed in locating the noisy bird, Ophelia hadn't heard him sneaking up on her. She'd always been fascinated with birds. She kept a journal of drawings of the different birds she had seen.

The man whose iron-like embrace she couldn't escape was brazen as the devil himself. Laying hands on her with a few hundred people within shouting distance. Which, no doubt, was why the first thing he'd done was render her incapable of calling for help.

Arching her back and craning her neck, she tried to see who held her captive. She didn't even have a hat pin or parasol to use as a weapon. More was the pity. That oversight would be remedied at once. Never again would she leave home without a means of protection, even if it was nothing more than a letter opener.

Clawing at his hand over her mouth, she screamed.

Only a muffled noise emerged.

"Hold still," the man hissed, dragging her farther away from the encampment. "I'm not going to hurt you."

Was he insane?

Did he think she'd believe anything he said?

Stanford. Where are you?

Why hadn't she listened to him?

Well, honestly, she didn't think anyone was

foolhardy enough to set upon her in broad daylight. She stomped on her assailant's foot, earning a grunt of pain as she dug the heel of her half boot into his arch.

"I knew you were a spirited woman." He sniffed her hair and pawed a breast. "I saw the way you looked at me. The lust in your pretty eyes, just like Lady Jamesworth."

Good Lord. Snooty, proper to her nose-in-the-air, overly-plucked eyebrows, Lady Elvina Jamesworth?

"But I told her ladyship I couldn't oblige her carnal needs today. She was most disappointed. How could I, when a fresh, innocent English Rose such as yourself gave me such a blatant invitation? So why are you struggling now? Do you like to pretend to resist?"

Ophelia went slack for a few heartbeats.

The wrestler?

Was he the wrestler who'd made her uncomfortable earlier?

How could she possibly hope to escape *him*?

He was a mass of muscles and strength.

Ophelia attempted to communicate that he was mistaken. She'd only been shocked to see a half-clothed man for the first time. She shook her head, and a few more tresses plopped onto her shoulders. Her bonnet had fallen to her back during the initial struggle, and several hairpins had slipped from her hair as well.

His harsh whisper seared her ear. "I know you, aloof English women. You flirt and then pretend resistance. It's your pride, I think. A Roma is beneath you, but you always find your pleasure *beneath* Django."

Shaking her head harder, Ophelia tried to bite his hand.

He laughed at her futile efforts.

"No. No," she mumbled against Django's palm. If only she could get an arm free, she could clobber him soundly. She knew how to swing a punch.

He chuckled again, the sound reverberating against her spine.

"My vardo is this way, pretty lady. It assures me privacy when I entertain," he continued as if they were having a discussion over tea and biscuits.

He made a harsh sound in the back of his throat.

"The same pampered ladies who lift their noses and

turn their backs in public are only too happy to sneak into my bed and spread their perfumed thighs. They moan their pleasure as I take them, begging for more. Never fear. Django knows how to please a woman."

His voice had grown gruffer, and something hard nudged Ophelia's bottom.

Dear God.

Was she about to be ravished?

All because her curiosity had led her astray?

Please, God. Help me, and I swear I'll never be imprudent again. That is, I'll try not to be, Ophelia quickly amended, not wanting to lie to the Almighty and knowing herself too well.

Renewing her struggles, she jerked her head back, trying to connect with her abductor's chin. Stinging tears filled her eyes as he yanked her hair.

"Stop that. Why do you struggle so? I am only giving you what you wanted, sweetheart."

All the while, the stupid bird squawked and screeched.

A movement beyond the trees sent Ophelia's heart stampeding with hope.

Stanford.

"Ophelia," Stanford roared, dropping the mugs he'd been carrying and sprinting toward her. His hat flew off his raven head as he raced in her direction. Fury slashed his brows together, and pure menace etched his face.

Django spotted Stanford too.

"Unhand my betrothed," Stanford shouted. "I'll kill you for touching her."

"*Khul,*" Django spat with such ferocity that Ophelia had no doubt he'd said something vulgar. "Shit, see what you have done, witch?"

He released her, shoving her hard so that she stumbled and fell to her knees and hands.

Ophelia cried out as stones cut into her skin. Her hair fell in great tangles to her shoulders and flopped forward, the ends brushing the dirt. She had no doubt she looked like a woman thoroughly compromised.

Oh, God. In Society's eyes, she *was* compromised.

"I pity you, English," Django scoffed. "She's a frigid wench. I'm fortunate my bollocks didn't freeze off swiving her."

Scorching chagrin heated Ophelia's face at his

crudity and the horrendous implication of his slur.

"Shut your filthy mouth, you unworthy cur," Stanford snarled, baring his teeth.

Django might be a champion wrestler, but given the fury fairly radiating off Stanford, Ophelia wouldn't wager the gypsy would win a fight between the two men.

Evidently, Django surmised the same. With a crude gesture and a mocking laugh, he took off. His heavy footfalls echoed through the now eerily silent woods.

The blasted annoying bird had finally shut up.

Struggling to rise, Ophelia winced as her stinging hands and knees objected. She glanced down, not surprised to see blood staining her white gloves. When she looked up again, her heart vaulted to her throat.

Stanford bore down upon her, his face ravaged with murderous fury.

She fell backward onto her bottom, throwing an arm up to shield herself from his wrath.

"No," she cried.

Astonishment and then hurt skittered across his features when he realized she feared him. Behind him, several other people ran into the copse.

Including, God help her, Maxwell and Gabriella.

They must've heard the shouting.

Gulping, she closed her eyes.

This wasn't good. Not good at all.

Stanford skidded to a halt. Little bits of dirt and debris pelted her ruined skirt. It didn't matter. Dampness beneath her knees told her they bled as well, and the gown was probably beyond repair.

"Ophelia?" Ragged and uncertain, his voice was the merest whisper of sound. "Ophelia?" he said again.

Reluctantly, she opened her eyes.

He crouched before her, his eyes crinkled with sorrow and yet still flashing with restrained raged.

"Are you hurt?" His attention fell to her bloodied gloves, and he flexed his jaw. "I'll kill him."

He spoke the words matter of factly.

"No, Stanford. He's not worth it. I wouldn't have that on my conscience or yours for that matter." Ophelia shifted her focus over his shoulder, and she bit her lower lip. "I fear we have a far more inconvenient problem."

She tried to smile, but her lips refused to curve

upward. In fact, they began to tremble uncontrollably. And then, to her horror, big tears slipped from her eyes.

"Oh, darling. Please don't cry." Stanford kneeled and gathered her into his arms. And it felt marvelous and safe and as if she belonged there. "Shh, I'm here. All shall be well, my little dove."

"No," she mumbled into his delicious-smelling shirt, refusing to look up. "It shan't. Look behind you."

Stanford glanced over his shoulder. His muscles grew taut, and she knew he'd realized the peril of their predicament. Though entirely innocent on their part, it appeared otherwise.

"Damnation," he murmured beneath his breath.

Damnation indeed.

"I'm sorry, Ophelia," he whispered into her ear.

For swearing or for the quandary they found themselves in?

"Fee Fee," Gabriella cried, rushing forward as Stanford helped Ophelia stand. "Oh, dearest, please tell me you are all right. I'll never forgive myself if you are hurt."

"I'm fine now, Gabby. Just a few cuts, scrapes, and

bruises." She permitted her sister to enfold her in a fragrant hug. "The Duke of Asherford rescued me."

"Yes. Yes. We saw everything." Gabriella's voice held an odd inflection. "And *heard,* as well."

What did she mean by that?

A buzz of whispers accompanied her declaration, and Ophelia wished the earth would part and swallow her.

"Asherford," Maxwell said in a low, urgent tone as he stepped near and turned his back to provide a small degree of privacy from the animated audience gathering behind them. "I hope you were serious when you claimed for all and sundry to hear that Ophelia is your betrothed. She's ruined if that isn't true."

Ruined?

It was dashed unfair.

Stanford glanced at Ophelia, a question burning in his blue eyes.

"Are you?" he silently asked.

Swallowing the lump of shock and angst clogging her throat, Ophelia stood stock-still as she felt the color drain from her face.

She would have to marry Stanford, Duke of Asherford.

There was nothing for it.

How he must be reveling in the turn of events which forced her hand. She would be his. And yet, all she detected in his expression and eyes was compassion and regret.

"The Duke of Asherford asked for my hand weeks ago," Ophelia said, astonished at how strong and even her voice sounded when her heart was shattering behind her breastbone. He had asked, and with any luck, everyone present would assume she'd agreed to the match.

What woman didn't want to become a duchess?

Ophelia, for one.

Maxwell and Gabriella exchanged a startled glance that said, *He did? Why didn't we know about it?* Then their gazes came to rest upon her once more.

"And," Gabriella urged gently. "What did you say?"

Ophelia knew Gabriella was only trying to protect her by making her claim publicly that she and the duke were affianced, but she wasn't sure Ophelia could say the words aloud. Once she did, her fate was nearly sealed. Breaking a betrothal to a duke was no minor social infraction. She might as well take vows and cloister herself in a convent in France for the remainder of her life.

Stanford took her hand in his and then, mindful of her injured palm, tenderly raised her hand to his mouth. An encouraging half-smile bending his lips, he stared intently into her eyes, waiting for her to be the one to make the announcement.

No doubt others had heard his declaration that they were betrothed. Thus, Ophelia's reputation could be salvaged, and her ability to marry for love sacrificed with one tiny word.

Simultaneous salvation and crushed dreams.

She would exchange her freedom to choose her future for gilded imprisonment—all for the sake of her blasted reputation. Which, come to think of it, was really highly overrated.

Nonetheless, she knew what she must do, not only for her sake but also for his and Gabriella's and

Maxwell's. So Ophelia fashioned a brittle smile and permitted Stanford to tuck her hand into the crook of his elbow.

She inhaled deeply, then forced the word past her lips. "Yes."

6

Berkeley Square

Mayfair, London

20 June 1810

Two days later

S tan was betrothed to Ophelia Breckensole. They were to wed seven days hence.

He should be euphoric and celebrating his victory. Marriage to Ophelia was precisely what he'd wanted—what he'd striven to achieve for weeks. She would make an exceptional duchess.

His vibrant, intelligent, intriguing, lovely duchess.

Except, a joining under scandalous circumstances cast an oppressive pall over the union. He'd never know if she would've consented to be his bride willingly and of her own volition.

If naught else, Ophelia was pragmatic. Another trait Stan admired about her. She'd known from the moment she'd looked over his shoulder and seen the gathering crowd of titillated or shocked onlookers that her life had irreversibly changed.

The choice of whom she'd marry had been taken from her.

Oh, Pennington would've continued to provide for Ophelia. Stan hadn't a doubt about that, but *le beau monde* wasn't known for its benevolence. She would've become an outcast through no fault of her own.

Stan didn't believe curiosity about a noisy bird—he hadn't had the opportunity to tell her it was actually a raucous squirrel—deserved a tainted reputation and ostracism. The upper ten thousand were eager to judge others while those same prideful elites hid their myriad of sins. If that wasn't the height of hypocrisy, he didn't know what was.

Hadn't he used his knowledge of peers' *shortcomings* to his advantage? Never to the point of extortion or blackmail—he was a man of honor, after all. But a subtle hint did wonders to persuade a reckless earl or a spendthrift marquis to make good on their legal debts, usually from gambling. Debts which Stan had purchased for pennies on the pound and then collected the entire amount plus interest from the wastrels.

As the coach rounded a corner, he checked his timepiece. Pennington expected him at two of the clock to sign the settlement papers. Afterward, Stan would join the family and a few close friends to formally announce his betrothal to Ophelia.

Despite the circumstances compelling her to marry him, his pulse accelerated in anticipation of seeing Ophelia. He'd given her two days to recover from the incident on Gipsy Hill, though he'd sent flowers, sweetmeats, and a short note each day. And a pair of peach-faced green lovebirds yesterday.

Stan had no idea why he'd done the latter. But Ophelia had seemed so fascinated by the *"bird"* that had landed her in the mischief to start with, he thought she might enjoy the lovebirds.

He'd also used his reputation as The Dangerous Duke to partially stifle the gossip filtering around the clubs and upper salons about the incident. Not that the juicy tidbit could be eradicated entirely. The most he could hope to do was marginally temper the consequences.

Likewise, Stan had used the time to set a runner after the gypsy who'd accosted Ophelia. As expected, the blighter had left his tribe, and no one knew where he'd gone.

Rot and rubbish.

At least that was what the Bow Street Runner had been told upon questioning the Roma. The runner had discovered Django Bostock was the gypsy king's nephew and was well-liked amongst his clan. He was also the best wrestler in their troupe and brought in considerable funds from wagers on the outcome of his matches.

Stan would be bound that Bostock had merely gone ahead of his tribe and would await them somewhere along their usual route.

A few minutes later, a pleasant-faced butler invited him inside the house. The ivory marble floor, gilded frames, and bouquets of fresh flowers within the foyer bespoke Pennington's wealth in a tasteful, understated way.

"I am Reeves," the butler intoned as one confident of his rank and position. "His grace awaits you in the study. May I be the first of the staff to offer my congratulations on your upcoming nuptials?"

"Thank you, Reeves. I am a very fortunate man." Stan followed the short, stout butler who made up for his height with lofty self-importance.

"Indeed, sir. Most fortunate."

Reeves marched along, his focus straight forward, but Stan couldn't help but think the diminutive man had something pressing he wanted to say.

Reeves cleared his throat.

"Miss Ophelia is a rarity—a jewel among jewels. As beautiful on the inside as she is outwardly." Reverence and fond regard weighted the servant's words. "We all hope she is very happy as your duchess."

And there was a distinct warning in Reeves's carefully modulated tenor as well.

The Dangerous Duke would've taken umbrage at such impudence. Stan, however, did not. This new person he was attempting to become must be more tolerant and forgiving.

For a majordomo to speak thusly to a duke meant the man would risk his position out of loyalty and a desire to protect Ophelia. His devotion increased Stan's esteem for the man. It also suggested that the staff knew exactly why Ophelia was wedding so hastily.

He would have spared her that humiliation.

"I pray she is happy as well, Reeves. I shall do my utmost to see that she is."

Stopping before a closed door, Reeves gave a half-smile of approval and nodded once before rapping upon the wood. "Very good, Your Grace."

Well, at least Stan had the butler's endorsement.

"Enter," Pennington called.

Reeves opened the door. "The Duke of Asherford, Your Grace."

The study was decorated as expected for a peer. Polished dark walnut shelves contained a myriad of books and masculine novelties. A large pedestal desk situated between two floor-to-ceiling windows dominated the room. Before the desk, a pair of burgundy armchairs sitting at right angles flanked a mahogany end table.

Pennington glanced up, and his face lightened. "Come in, Asherford. Thank you, Reeves."

The butler backed out and closed the door softly behind him.

"I've been warned to make Ophelia happy," Stan said with a grin while flicking a glance toward the closed panel as he extended his hand.

Pennington clasped his palm and quirked a brow. "Have you, now?"

"Quite forthrightly, in truth," Stan admitted.

Chuckling, Pennington released Stan's hand and settled into the chair behind the desk. "Ophelia has that effect on people. Please sit. Make yourself comfortable? Brandy? Whisky? Something else?"

Pennington had never been this cordial to Stan before. But then again, they were soon to be brothers-in-law, so perhaps he'd decided to forge a friendship between them. As their wives were twins, they'd no doubt see a great deal of one another.

"No, thank you." Stan shook his head. "I shall await

refreshment until we join the women."

"Of course." Elbows on the desktop, Pennington steepled his fingers, his expression contemplative. "Before we get to the matter at hand, I would ask why I knew nothing of your marriage proposal to Ophelia?"

In truth, Stan had expected Ophelia would've shared his proposal with her sister.

"I asked her, and she turned me down. Flatly." Actually, acting like an arrogant arse, he'd announced they'd suit. She was right to have refused him. "I suppose she didn't think the offer deserved merit and therefore didn't feel the need to share or discuss it."

Pennington's eyebrows shied up his forehead. "She didn't breathe a word. Most unusual, since the twins share nearly everything."

Stan leaned forward. Suddenly, it was imperative that Pennington know how much he wanted to marry Ophelia. "From the moment I first met Ophelia, I was drawn to her. I acted the arse, however. Instead of wooing her, I *told* her we would suit and should marry. I may have listed her admirable attributes: acceptable lineage, adequate temperament, and decorum."

"You did not!" Pennington burst out laughing and slapped his desk. "Zounds, I'd love to have been there for that exchange."

Turning his mouth down and veeing his eyebrows in annoyance, Stan hooked an ankle over his knee.

"I'm glad my humiliation amuses you," he said in dry tones.

"Forgive me, Asherford. I understand you do not find the situation amusing. But you shall be spared much grief if you understand Ophelia doesn't like being told what to do." Pennington tapped his desk with a fingertip. "She's rather mulish that way and will dig her heels in out of sheer obstinacy. So will her sister."

"So I've learned." Stan's irritation evaporated. He had no reason to be peeved at Pennington for telling the truth. "Regardless, I'd decided to court her until I won her affections, but the incident at Gipsy Hill precludes that now."

"I shall be perfectly frank with you, Asherford. I think marrying you is the wisest thing Ophelia can do to deter gossip and save her reputation. Nonetheless, up until she says "I do," if she changes her mind, I'll support her in that decision." He tapped the small pile of documents stacked neatly atop his desk. "Marriage settlement or no. I've included just such a provision. I won't have you suing for breach of contract."

Insulted that Pennington would suggest something so dishonorable, ire stiffened Stan's spine and tightened his gut. After a heartbeat and a deep breath, he tamped down his anger. Pennington was merely protecting Ophelia. He meant no slight.

"I agree," Stan said. "I would not have Ophelia enter a forced marriage."

In short order, the documents had been reviewed and signed with one amendment. "I don't want Ophelia's dowry. Establish a trust for her. Then she can decide how to spend it."

Pennington arched a brow and skewed his mouth into a sideways smile. "That's most generous of you."

"Generosity has nothing to do with it. I want Ophelia to know that nothing compelled me to marry. Circumstances might force her to marry me, but the reverse is not true."

Pennington made an indecipherable sound and

scribbled a few lines on the document. He turned it to face Stan. "Will that suffice?"

Stan scanned the modification and nodded. "Yes. I also want her to know that the money is hers. I believe it will help her feel empowered in a situation that surely must make her feel powerless."

Leaning back into his leather chair, Pennington rubbed his chin. "Given your reputation for ruthlessness, I admit, I'm surprised at your consideration for Ophelia's feelings."

"She will be my wife. I shall always consider her feelings above all else."

A slow grin pulled Pennington's lips upward, and a devilish glint entered his eyes. "As it should be." He stood and gestured toward the closed door. "Shall we go find your bride and mine?"

My bride.

"By all means. I have a ring I wish to present to her." Stan patted his coat pocket. That was another thing he'd done these past two days. Shopped for the perfect ring. The duchy had few genuine jewels left. Most were paste imitations. Ophelia deserved a ring as unique and beautiful as she was.

"I shall arrange for you to have a few minutes alone," Pennington offered as they stepped into the hallway. "The other guests aren't due to arrive for half an hour. You may speak with Ophelia in the drawing room until a quarter of three."

Stan kept stride with Pennington as he led the way to the drawing room. They entered, and the Duchess of Pennington and Ophelia glanced up.

Today, they looked identical, except the duchess wore a rosy pink, and Ophelia wore periwinkle trimmed in violet. And while the duchess's expression was neutral but pleasant, Ophelia's was unreadable. As if she'd donned a mask, much like the one she'd worn the other night at the ball.

"My dear," Pennington said. "I've promised Asherford he might have a few moments alone with his betrothed before the other guests arrive."

Ophelia's gaze flew to meet Stan's before she swiftly dropped her attention to her tightly clasped hands.

A most reluctant bride.

His gut wrenched. Could he go through with the marriage when Ophelia so obviously didn't want to? The Dangerous Duke wouldn't have hesitated. But Stan didn't want to be that man anymore.

Ophelia had changed him.

No. She'd made him want to change.

That question echoed in Stan's mind as the duchess slid her sister an inquisitive glance. If Ophelia wanted her to stay, he had no doubt she would, despite her husband's polite request.

When Ophelia summoned a smile and a nod, her grace extended her hand toward Pennington. "I need to look in on Cook in any event. I've asked her to try a new recipe for lemon queen cakes. Theadosia vows they are the best she's ever tasted, but Cook was worried about the amount of lemon required. She feared they'd be bitter."

Theadosia was the Duke of Sutcliffe's wife. She was also a bosom friend of Ophelia and her twin. Stan made a point to know such details.

At the door, her grace turned. "We'll be back shortly, Ophelia. You aren't wed yet, and we don't want any more scandals. I shall leave the door open."

"Of course," Ophelia said, though color stained the delicate slope of her cheekbones.

The duke and duchess took their leave.

Stan waited until their footsteps faded in the corridor before he crossed the room and, after a slight hesitation, sat beside Ophelia on the navy-blue and gold silk striped settee.

"How are you, Ophelia? Have your cuts healed?"

"I am well, and yes, the cuts are little more than scratches now." She brushed a curl away from her ear. "Thank you for the lovebirds. Oh, and the chocolate and flowers, of course."

The indecipherable mask slipped away, her hazel eyes twinkled, and she grinned. No coy smiles or seductive upward sweep of her lips. Ophelia expressed emotions without artifice.

"The birds are in my chamber. They are the sweetest pair, Your Grace. I've named them Orsino and Viola from Shakespeare's *Twelfth Night*."

"But didn't Orsino love Olivia while Viola secretly loved him?" Stan teased. "And he thought she was a man to boot?"

Ophelia pulled a playful face at him. "I refused to name them something as cliché as Romeo and Juliet."

"Or Cleopatra and Antony?" he quipped.

"Indeed not. Those tragic characters killed themselves."

Tilting her head at an endearing angle, she narrowed her eyes in mock retribution.

"If you're not careful, Your Grace, I shall name them something genuinely horrendous like Englebert and Ernestine. Or Hildegarde and Hortensio."

"Enough of that 'Your Grace' nonsense," Stan gently admonished. What would she do if he pulled her onto his lap? No. It was best to wait until she was less skittish. "We are to be wed. You know my name and have used it before. I would not have that formality between us."

Her expression grew mischievous, and she giggled. "Or I could name the birds Frederick and Florencia."

Stan chuckled and then formed an artificial scowl

of disapproval. Pretending affront, he said in his most imperious tone, "I'll have you know, one of my middle names is Frederick."

"I know," she said, then lowered her voice to a solemn tone. "Stanford Julius Frederick Bancroft, Duke of Asherford. My name is much prettier. Ophelia Audrey Summer Breckensole."

At that moment, a piece of his hard heart melted. He'd wrongly believed Ophelia would be sullen or cross, or, at the very least, despondent about their upcoming nuptials. But, instead, she jested with him.

"You are a remarkable woman, Ophelia Audrey Summer Breckensole."

He bent his head and whisked a kiss across her smiling pink lips.

Going perfectly still, she inhaled sharply but didn't pull away.

Her perfume, bergamot and orange blossoms, and perhaps a hint of vanilla, wrapped around his senses in a heady miasma. She smelled incredible, and it took all of his willpower not to nuzzle her neck and lick the tender flesh there to see if she tasted as good as she smelled.

Stan cupped her cheek and kissed her again, lingering a trifle longer this time. Sweet didn't begin to describe the taste of her mouth. Desire was too placid a word to define the raging inferno that had erupted in his blood at the touch of her lips against his.

Stan had chosen Ophelia to be his bride for rational reasons. He hadn't expected all-consuming passion to overtake him with one kiss. That reaction wasn't logical or practical.

Mindful that the Penningtons were due to return shortly and that sporting a cockstand mightn't be the best way to ingratiate himself into the good graces of his future in-laws, he drew back.

Mouth slightly parted and delightfully red, Ophelia searched his eyes. "Why did you kiss me?"

"Because you tempt me beyond self-control, my little dove."

"I thought you were always in control."

What an odd thing to say, and a great misperception too.

"I'm flattered you should think so," Stan said. "I strive for that appearance." He paused, then shook his head, his expression rueful and a trifle self-conscious. "No, I used to endeavor for that. No longer."

She cocked her head. "Why?"

Grinning, he kissed her nose. "That discussion cannot be completed in the time we have before your sister and Pennington return. It will have to wait until another time. I want to give you this before they do."

He withdrew the box from his pocket and opened the purple velvet top. Inside, resting in a white satin nest, lay a pear-shaped amethyst ring surrounded by white diamonds and an outer layer of opals, all nestled in a gold setting.

"Oh," Ophelia gasped in delight. "It's stunning, Stanford. How did you know purple is my favorite color and opals are my favorite gemstone?"

He relaxed against the settee, draping an arm over the carved back. "I asked your sister. I wanted you to have a ring that meant something to you personally and not just a family heirloom."

A paste one, at that. Stan would have to buy jewels for Ophelia and restock the duchy's cache.

"Would you put it on me, please?" She held out her

long, slender fingers with a neat oval fingernail on the tip of each.

After he'd obliged, Stan cradled her hand in his. For a few moments, he searched for the right words. Words that wouldn't offend or seem trivial. Words that conveyed the importance of this moment and that would encourage her. *Thank you for accepting my proposal* was grossly inadequate. As was his wont, he settled on pragmatism.

"I believe we can be happy together, Ophelia."

"I, ah, wanted to discuss something with you." She averted her glance, and a rosy hue tinged her cheeks.

"Yes?" he gently prompted.

Typically, she was straightforward. This diffidence was uncharacteristic, and warning bells sounded in Stan's mind.

She squared her shoulders and met his gaze directly.

There was the Ophelia he knew and esteemed.

In a rush, she blurted, "Since our union is so hasty, and we don't really know each other, and we are being forced into the marriage, I think we should wait to consummate our vows."

8

Fingers squeezed tight, Ophelia held her breath, waiting for Stanford's response. She'd rehearsed what she wanted to say. That nervous, stumbling-over-her-tongue jumble hadn't been the smooth, rational speech she'd practiced.

Regardless, her meaning was clear, and Stanford would have to be as obtuse and as thick as a one-hundred-year-old oak's trunk to not comprehend her meaning. He was neither of those things.

It was incomprehensible to consider physical intimacy with a man she scarcely knew. She had no idea what his food preferences were or if he had any pets or favorite activities. What was more, she didn't know what Stanford *didn't* like, although his reputation suggested nearly everything fell into that category.

Her soon-to-be husband wasn't known for his good nature and genial mien.

But still, shouldn't husbands and wives at least know each other's favorite color or how many children they wanted? And that intrusive thought brought her right back to the issue at hand.

Consummating their vows.

Folding her hands together, Ophelia darted a swift glance to the mantel clock.

Two forty-two.

Gabriella and Maxwell would return any moment.

Perhaps she ought to have waited to make her request, but she'd been a bundle of nerves since arriving at the decision early this morning after having lain awake all night. She wasn't saying she and Stanford would never consummate the marriage.

Just not right away.

Only a couple of days ago, she'd vowed to never wed him.

She still hadn't adjusted to the fact that in one week, he would be her husband. In truth, she had considered reneging and letting scandal reign. But every time she examined the consequences of that decision, it brought her full circle.

A compromised woman wasn't welcome in Society. She'd face malicious whispers and unwanted attention from men who now believed her fast and a wanton. By marrying Stanford and becoming a duchess, she might suffer a few unkind looks and cuts, but a duchess was powerful in her own right.

This wasn't the path Ophelia would've chosen, but moping about all Friday faced would serve no purpose. *She* had wandered farther into the woods, out of sight of Stanford and the fair-goers, and had been caught unawares. The responsibility lay solely at her feet, even if the consequences were unjust.

The weighty silence seemed to drag on forever. She glanced at the clock again, resisting the urge to wiggle or prod him into responding.

Two forty-four.

"How long?" Stanford asked, rubbing the bridge of his nose. Nothing in his tone gave away his emotions.

Ophelia's gaze flew to his.

He was actually considering her request?

Without arguing?

Wetting her lower lip, she blinked rather stupidly at him.

Ophelia had hoped he would, of course, but she hadn't expected he'd be this cooperative. In fact, she'd anticipated a battle. Quite a loud, intense, highly unpleasant argument, truth be told. She was far more accustomed to quarrelsome encounters with Stanford than cooperation.

"I...well...honestly, I don't know." She hadn't thought that far ahead.

What was a reasonable amount of time to get to know one's spouse?

Several of her friends had fallen in love swiftly. Everleigh, Duchess of Sheffield, Theadosia, Duchess of Sutcliffe, Jessica, the new Duchess of Bainbridge, and Gabriella too. Gabriella said that her heart knew Maxwell was her soulmate, and waiting months or years to wed would've been ridiculous.

And Gabriella had loathed Maxwell before she fell tea kettle over bum in love with him.

Love was a strange creature, indeed. Not the least bit logical or sensible. Not that Ophelia expected to love Stanford. But mutual respect that mayhap developed into genuine liking wasn't too much to ask for, was it?

Footsteps echoed in the hallway, and Stanford slid a tense glance toward the open door.

"One month, Ophelia."

"A month?" The two words sounded strangled to her ears.

Was that long enough to get to know him? To feel comfortable sharing intimacies with him?

Feeling oddly shy, she peeked up at Stanford through her eyelashes. Their kiss had been astonishingly pleasant. At least for her. She presumed from his husky voice and reluctance to end the kiss that it had been for him as well.

"Can we discuss it again in a month if I'm still not ready?" she persisted, rather astonished at her tenacity.

Maxwell strode into the drawing room, her beaming sister on his arm. From Gabriella's flushed face and the masculine satisfaction in Maxwell's eyes, they'd done more than venture to the kitchen.

"Yes," Stanford said beneath his breath before facing them.

Ophelia squeezed the fingers of the hand lying on his thigh.

"Thank you," she murmured for his ears alone.

His answering, smoldering smile could've melted iron.

Ophelia skillfully avoided any awkward questions from her sister and Maxwell by holding up her hand and showing off the betrothal ring.

"Isn't it lovely?" Ophelia angled her hand to better catch the light. "Thank you for helping Stanford by telling him my favorite color and gemstone."

"Oh, it is beautiful." Gabriella took Ophelia's hand in hers to examine the ring closely. "Don't give me any credit. Asherford made the inquiry. He wanted to please you."

Gabriella gave Stanford a warm smile that clearly conveyed how much that meant to her.

Reeves entered carrying a tea service, followed by a pair of footmen bearing additional teapots and cups. Three maids brought up the rear with trays of dainties, sandwiches, sweetmeats, and cakes. The small betrothal party wasn't to be so very small after all.

Was that to put rumors to rest?

Likely. Not that the most devout gossips would stop wagging their malicious tongues.

The servants went about setting up the room for the guests that would arrive any minute. The adjoining music room double doors were opened to allow for more guests, and additional chairs had already been brought into both rooms.

Just how many *close* friends had Gabriella invited, anyway?

Ophelia's twin must've sensed her reticence because she offered a sympathetic smile. "It's what needs done, darling."

"I know," Ophelia replied.

She did know, and usually, she relished large gatherings.

Most of their friends from her hometown of Colchester were in London for the Season, including Ophelia's dearest newlywed friend Jessica Rolston, the Duchess of Bainbridge. Jessica had recently returned from her honeymoon.

Ophelia couldn't wait to see her. She'd married under the shadow of a scandal too. But Jessica had secretly been in love with Crispin, Duke of Bainbridge.

Ophelia was not in love with Stanford.

9

An hour later, Ophelia's face threatened to crack under the strain of constant smiling and pretending to be thrilled about her upcoming nuptials. Yet, her responses must've been believable because no one seemed to notice the tension radiating from her. Or the slight twitch that had begun at the corner of her mouth fifteen minutes ago.

In truth, that might be blamed on over-taxed muscles. In fact, that was the excuse Ophelia intended to use if anyone commented on the nervous tic.

A few minutes ago, she'd slipped out the French windows to the terrace adjacent to the drawing room. She couldn't stay away for long. She'd be missed, and that would cause more gossip.

Nonetheless, she desperately needed five minutes alone to calm her thoughts and to regain her equanimity. This nervousness sluicing through her was as foreign and unpleasant as the Russian caviar she'd sampled at the Berkenshires' rout a fortnight ago.

Chin tucked to her chest, she trailed a finger across a peach rosebud. The gardens weren't extensive but sufficed as a pleasant reprieve to enjoy nature.

Several times since the guests had arrived, she'd met Stanford's gaze from across the room. At first, she'd been relieved they wouldn't be forced together the entire afternoon. She hadn't been sure she could pull off the charade of a happy bride-to-be with him beside her. But astonishingly, she found herself seeking him out with her gaze, over and over, and wishing he was at her side.

Which, truth be told, was the queerest of things.

Since when had he become an ally?

Better an ally for a husband than an enemy.

Stanford had given her tender half-smiles, his blue eyes gleaming with something Ophelia couldn't name but which made her feel warm and feminine. At once, she felt rejuvenated and reassured—her nerves temporarily calmed. Which made no sense at all because *he* was the reason she was a taut, confused mess.

In a matter of days, her plans for her life had been wrested out of her control. She should resent it more than she did—she should resent Stanford. Only she couldn't. He'd given her the choice whether to wed him or not yesterday. She'd made the decision to acknowledge the faux betrothal as a reality.

Standing before the small burbling fountain surrounded by multi-colored freesia and ranunculus, she closed her eyes and touched a fingertip to her lips. Their kiss had been splendid…breathtaking.

Nothing like the two—*no, three*—rushed pecks by her other would-be suitors. Those had made her want to gag and clobber the brash young men.

Ophelia could still feel Stanford's mouth upon hers. Still smell his manly essence.

He'd proven more willing to compromise than she would've ever guessed.

Had she misjudged him all this time?

"I believe we can be happy together, Ophelia."

A private smile bent her mouth upward. Mayhap, just mayhap, they could be.

Feeling decidedly more cheerful than she had before sneaking from her betrothal party and humming a nonsensical little tune as she imagined what life as Stanford's wife would be like, she retraced her steps.

"There *you* are."

Ophelia jerked her head up.

Bother and rot.

Just what Ophelia did not need.

Candace Metcalfe.

And, naturally, her constant shadow and cohort, Ann Marie Washburne, accompanied her.

"I saw you sneak out." Candace gave Ann Marie a side-eyed superior glance. As if she'd caught Ophelia in a criminal act and gloated about her discovery.

"Yes, we saw you," Anne Marie put in with a swift glance for approval toward Candace. "Sneak out, that is."

As usual, Candace ignored her.

Ophelia hadn't thought anyone had seen her slip out the French doors.

She raised an eyebrow and stared the viper down. "It's hardly sneaking to take a bit of air in my brother-in-law's garden."

"I never would've thought you would stoop so low as to entrap a duke, Ophelia Breckensole. But then, how else could a country bumpkin snare Asherford?" Blond eyebrows and not so dainty nose elevated, Candace scraped a scathing gaze over Ophelia. "You are certainly not duchess material," she said in her snide, singsong tenor.

She possessed a voice that could curdle milk from another room. It grated along a person's spine and made one want to stick one's fingers in one's ears.

Or stuff a throw pillow in Candace's rouged mouth.

Ophelia suspected Candace had affected the tone after much practice, with the mistaken belief that she sounded elegant. However, her mother had much the same whiney inflection. One would think they'd notice the swift retreat of anyone within proximity when they spoke, but the two women were as thick as week-old porridge.

Candace would've been beautiful with her golden

blond hair and pale blue eyes if it wasn't for her perpetual pout.

Ann Marie giggled, covering her buckteeth with a pudgy hand. She shadowed Candace and mimicked her unkind behavior. No wonder Candace was her only friend.

"Oh, Candace," Ann Marie said. "You are too bad. You shouldn't call anyone a bumpkin. Mama refers to country folk with no breeding as clod poles. It's kinder and less offensive."

She turned an artificial smile toward Ophelia as if she expected to be thanked for her compassion. Comparing Ann Marie's acumen to a parsnip's was an insult to the root vegetable.

Why were either of the young women here?

They assuredly were not friends of the Penningtons or of Ophelia. She highly doubted they ranked high on Stanford's acquaintance list either.

No doubt, a mutual friend had mentioned the occasion, and Candace and Ann Marie had taken it upon themselves to tag along. Audacious on their part. Gabriella was too well-mannered to make a scene and toss them out, but she'd make sure they never presumed to overstep again.

When several of one's friends were duchesses, a word here or there in the right ear could see an impudent young lady—or, in this case, ladies—booted to the *haut ton's* fringes. Especially when the disagreeable pair arrived with claws and teeth bared and were prepared to scratch one of the guests of honor.

Ophelia glanced over their shoulders toward the house, hoping someone else had noticed the trio on the terrace and might venture outdoors too.

She wasn't that lucky.

Regardless, she refused to be baited. These two hellcats wanted to draw a little blood because neither of them had any chance of landing Stanford. Or any other man of station, to be perfectly frank. Gentlemen with common sense avoided them as they would a leper.

"If you'll excuse me. My betrothed is no doubt wondering where I have gone." Yes, Ophelia felt the merest swell of pride when she said betrothed. It was very wicked of her, but she enjoyed the peeved scrunching of Candace's winged eyebrows.

"You do seem to make a habit of prowling about out of doors alone, Miss Breckensole. One might begin to question why?" Candace made a pretense of perusing the neatly trimmed shrubberies. "Or *are* you alone?"

The garden was so small, any man would've been clearly visible as the snide wench well knew. Refusing to give the snit the satisfaction of defending herself, Ophelia merely arched an eyebrow.

"Your affianced is in the house, is he not?" Ann Marie chirped in imitation of her friend.

Ophelia stared at her.

Dimwitted nincompoop.

"I just said as much," Ophelia said, struggling to keep the impatience from her voice.

"That's how she met that gypsy everyone is gossiping about, Candace. Creeping around the trees and shrubs," Ann Marie said with another annoying giggle. "Lady Jamesworth claims some of them are quite handsome in an uncivilized way. Why, they've even approached her ladyship with improper offers."

Ophelia barely restrained her snort of laughter.

Django had specifically mentioned Lady

Jamesworth as one of his…

What did one call such a woman?

A paramour?

Lover?

Strumpet?

Well, at least now Ophelia knew who the two irritating girls had come with. Lord Jamesworth was a close associate of Maxwell's. A kind man with soulful eyes that reminded Ophelia of a sad hound dog, he was thirty years older than his frivolous, loose-moraled wife if he was a day. Lady Jamesworth played the man for a fool, and yet he remained devoted to her.

"Please excuse me," Ophelia said. "I see that my hem is torn, and I need to repair it before rejoining the others."

It was true and provided just the excuse Ophelia needed to be rid of these pests. Rather than enter through the drawing room and risk Candace and Ann Marie creating a scene, Ophelia moved toward another French window farther down the flagstone.

She had no intention of changing her gown or sewing the hem straightaway. Let them think she meant to. Ophelia owed neither woman an explanation.

"Word has it, you were compromised, Miss Breckensole," Candace said. "Several respectable people witnessed your…dishabille and disgrace."

"Compromised, indeed." Ann Marie giggled again, reminding Ophelia of the hares common in the countryside. Had she sucked her thumb for too many years? Is that what had caused her protruding teeth?

Dressed in an unbecoming orange and bright blue gown, far too tight for her plump figure, the unfortunate girl resembled the parrot she sounded like.

No doubt Lady Jamesworth was responsible for spreading that ugly tarradiddle.

"Asherford, being the honorable gentleman that he is, fell for your harlot's ploy." Candace curled her mouth into an unbecoming sneer. She jabbed her pointer finger toward Ophelia. "*You* don't deserve him. He's far above you. You're little more than a common who—"

"That is quite enough, Miss Metcalfe."

The frigid, clipped words caused Candace to gasp and whirl around.

Stanford towered over them, displeasure stamped

onto his lean features. Blue sparks flew from his black-lashed eyes. "I shan't tolerate you insulting my betrothed."

Engrossed in refraining from slapping Candace's face, Ophelia hadn't heard Stanford approach either.

Her heart raced in gratitude and chagrin. Lips pressed into a tight ribbon, she met his furious blue eyes. She'd seen him angry before. Nevertheless, this rigidly controlled rage raised the hair on her nape and caused goose pimples to spring up along her arms.

Stanford regarded Candace with the same contempt he might fresh cow dung clinging to his polished Wellingtons.

"Y…your…Gr…ace," Candace stuttered, her complexion waxen. "You…you misunderstand."

Ann Marie had turned an unbecoming shade of puce. Her unremarkable brown eyes bugging from her head, she gasped like a banked trout, and little wheezing noises came from her slack mouth.

"I believe I understand perfectly," Stanford responded with a contemptuous glance over Candace's person. "You are a mean-spirited, jealous harpy. You delight in putting others down because it makes you feel better about yourself."

"That is true," Ann Marie whispered beneath her breath.

Candace leveled her a murderous glare meant to eviscerate.

Expression horrified, Ann Marie clapped her hand over her mouth. "I didn't mean it, Candace," she mumbled behind her fingers.

Eyes narrowed to hostile slits, Candace said, "Oh, I think *you* did."

Ann Marie frantically shook her head.

Candace would make her pay dearly for her slip.

Stanford held out his arm toward Ophelia. "Come, my darling. Let us return to the house. Pennington wants to raise a toast in our honor and wish us felicitations on our upcoming nuptials."

Head high and shoulders squared, Ophelia swept to his side without looking at the two sulking women.

Stanford tucked her hand into the crook of his elbow and covered it with his other hand. Bestowing a doting smile upon her, he leaned down and whispered into her ear. "I am going to kiss you on the forehead. I don't want those jealous twits to have any doubts as to my eagerness to wed you."

He proceeded to press his firm, warm lips to Ophelia's forehead in the tenderest of gestures.

Swiftly stifled gasps at his public display of affection caused Ophelia to curve her lips upward.

Well done, Stanford.

"Let's return indoors, my dear," he said. "The others await us."

She smiled up at him, somewhat dazed.

This Stanford, Duke of Asherford, was quite nice. Quite nice indeed.

At the door, he turned and swept a disdainful glance over Candace and Ann Marie, who still stood in chagrined shock.

"Lest you are tempted to spread gossip or defame my bride further, heed my warning. *Do. Not.*" He slashed his dark eyebrows together in the manner that had made him infamous.

Both girls swallowed audibly.

Stanford pressed on mercilessly. "The

repercussions would be dire for you both and any hopes you entertain of continuing in Society."

Drawing near until their shoulders bumped, Candace and Ann Marie clasped hands. Terror etched their features, and if Ophelia had been feeling charitable, she might've felt pity for them.

She wasn't feeling the least charitable, but neither did she revel at their fear.

They'd brought Stanford's wrath upon themselves, and now they could deal with the consequences.

"I proposed to Ophelia weeks ago."

He bathed Ophelia with such an adoring glance, she regretted the look was a farce for Candace's and Ann Marie's benefit.

"I consider it the greatest honor of my life that she has consented to be my bride," Stanford said with conviction. "I shan't take kindly to any further aspersions on her character. I shall consider it a personal insult. Do I make myself clear?"

Eyes round and unblinking, the women nodded.

"Excellent."

He slipped an arm around Ophelia's waist as if

laying claim to her. The heat of his arm branded her. Even while her mind pondered why she didn't object, her body melded closer to his.

Stanford opened the door. "Come, my love."

At that moment, Ophelia almost believed he meant the words.

10

Kenclere Hall

Near Oxfordshire, England

27 June 1810

Late afternoon

From beneath hooded lashes, Stan regarded his wife of nine hours.

Ophelia was exquisite in her turquoise and black traveling costume, with jet earrings dangling from her ears. The lovebirds he'd given her perched in their cage on the seat beside her. She'd covered their cage with a cloth to keep them calm during the journey.

Every now and again, one would chirp or ruffle its feathers, and its mate would answer. He'd been told when he purchased them that they had been a pair for just under a year.

"Did you know that lovebirds mate for life?" he asked.

Ophelia gave him a startled look, then glanced at the cage and smiled. "I did. I think it's sweet."

Unlike birds in the wild, these lovebirds hadn't chosen each other as mates. And yet, like their wild counterparts, they'd remain faithful and loving until one of them died.

It was the oddest thing, but that little tidbit gave Stan reason to hope that he and Ophelia might find happiness together. He wasn't fool enough to hope for love. In truth, Stan wasn't sure he believed in love.

His parents' union had been an arranged marriage. His mother had died in childbirth when he was three, after giving birth to a stillborn daughter. Stan had been left in the care of servants and tutors until his sire's death on the dueling field.

The previous Duke of Asherford had not been discreet when it came to his lovers. He'd cuckolded the wrong man and found himself on the deadly end of a dueling pistol.

"How do you tell them apart?" Stan was eager to keep Ophelia conversing.

She had been unduly meditative and quiet as she sat opposite him. Several times, he'd seen her smooth forehead furrow or her plump lips turn down. Nonetheless, not once had she complained about anything.

"Orsino feeds Viola." She grinned. "Apparently, that old wives' tale about the way to a man's heart being through his stomach is the opposite for lovebirds."

Stan recalled a similar thought he'd had about Ophelia that day at Gipsy Hill.

Ophelia patted the top of the cage. "I hope they have babies. I think it would be splendid to have several lovebirds flying around a conservatory." Giving a self-conscious laugh, she folded her hands in her lap and crossed her trim ankles. "I presume one of your estates has a conservatory."

"They do. I have three, in truth as well as an orangery and a pinery."

"You grow pineapples?" she asked, awestruck.

Stan chuckled. "I don't, but my gardener does."

Ophelia made a soft little humming noise before retreating into silence again, her focus somewhere beyond the window.

As much as Stan thought he knew about his new duchess, he'd realized this past week that his bride was an enigma to him in many ways.

That was perfectly all right. He and Ophelia had a lifetime to get to know each other through and through. Seeing that she was happy and content topped his lists of priorities. Just below protecting her.

She shifted slightly, and a soft, almost imperceptible sigh escaped her.

What was she thinking?

Regretting their marriage already?

The noble thing to do would be to turn the coach around and have the marriage annulled. But Stan was a selfish bastard. He'd wanted Ophelia to be his duchess, and now that she was, only death would separate them.

His ribs contracted with sadness at her pensiveness before he tamped the useless emotion down. Ophelia would come 'round. Kenclere Hall was a vast and beautiful estate. One of four Stan owned—five if he counted the hunting lodge on the Scottish border.

He planned on introducing her to all of them eventually.

In all likelihood, her somber mood was due as much to leaving her sister as entering into a rushed marriage. Theirs wasn't a forced or arranged marriage, but neither had it been a love match. Stan had never anticipated marrying for love, but Ophelia was a romantic.

He knew that much about her. That was why he fully intended to keep wooing her.

Following a small wedding by way of a special license at the Penningtons' house and a sumptuous breakfast, Ophelia had tearfully bid her twin farewell.

Other than the Duke and Duchess of Pennington's honeymoon, the sisters had never been apart for any length of time. Stan had decided it best if he and his new bride began their lives together away from London and the tattle still filtering around *le beau monde* regarding their rushed marriage.

It wouldn't be long until a new scandal took center stage, and the reason for his and Ophelia's hasty marriage was forgotten. He had another much more pressing reason for wanting her away from London, however.

The first note had been waiting for Stan when he'd returned home from the betrothal party.

So, you are to be married.
You think you deserve happiness?
After you've destroyed so many lives?
Sleep with a lamp burning, Your Grace.

Unsurprisingly, there had been no return address. When Stanford had questioned his butler about the missive, Atherton had furrowed his substantial beetle brows. "A street lad delivered it after you departed this afternoon. The boy scampered off before I could ask him who sent it. He seemed quite frightened, Your Grace."

Three more notes had arrived since, and each time, the urchin raced off before he could be questioned. The last had literally tossed the missive on the floor the instant Atherton had opened the door.

Each letter contained subtle threats. Whoever was

sending them knew enough about Stan and Ophelia to raise his alarm. Out of fear for Ophelia's safety, he'd determined a stay at Kenclere Hall, his grand country house, was in order.

Never one to take unnecessary chances, he'd put the word out that they were honeymooning in Northumberland. His harasser would find themselves on a wild goose chase should they journey there. Taking Ophelia's safety one step further, he'd asked the small number of people who knew they were at Kenclere Hall to keep that knowledge to themselves.

A determined sort could easily discover the whereabouts of Stan's estates, but honestly, it had been some time since he'd made a new enemy. One of his old adversaries might be out to exact revenge, but only a few of them still owed him a balance for their outstanding debts.

In fact, he'd forgiven the remainder of Lord Lionel Willoughby-Elliot's debt with the birth of the chap's sixth daughter. With that many daughters to dower and marry off, Willoughby-Elliot had been most grateful for the reprieve and vowed to never gamble again.

Hopefully, he'd keep his word.

Stan had also contacted the Bow Street Runner still searching for Django Bostock without luck and asked him to hire two men to watch Stan's Grosvenor Square house and another three to monitor Kenclere Hall. Not one to take chances, he'd sent word ahead to Kenclere Hall and had Filson, the majordomo, hire a half dozen men from the village to act as guards.

They were to pretend to be gardeners and laborers around the estate so that Ophelia would not become alarmed or suspicious. The seven footmen in residence at Kenclere Hall had been advised to be alert and have a weapon ready should the need arise.

In truth, Stan didn't think there was any real peril. Over the past decade, he'd received many hot-winded threats. Always from frustrated and angry wastrels, whose debts he'd purchased and demanded payment for.

It never ceased to astonish him how many peers felt it perfectly acceptable to run up gambling and other substantial debts and then believe themselves too lofty and privileged to honor their obligations. He hadn't restored the duchy's coffers by permitting those who owed him monies to continue with that delusion.

Regardless, Stan wasn't entirely without a heart. No man with a family had been put out of his only home, although Stan had acquired multiple deeds to other dwellings jackanapes had gambled away. Yes, some irresponsible lords and other elites had been forced to sell their horses, carriages, jewels, and other valuables to pay their debts.

But none had been put out on the street, and all had food to fill their family's bellies.

In recent years, Stan had stopped buying the debts of others. He'd made enough enemies to last a lifetime, and he didn't enjoy his reputation as The Dangerous Duke. Unfortunately, given his tendency toward dourness and cynicism, the label had stuck. He'd resigned himself to living with the unflattering moniker.

With diligent management of his estates, he had obtained enough wealth and felt the duchy's future was secure. That didn't mean there hadn't been uncomfortable moments when he'd run into a peer at a social gathering whose debt Stan had called in. There had been many, in truth. He always approached it as a business arrangement: professional, unemotional, and detached.

That was probably why he'd been accused of having *bloody ice* in his veins several times.

But being a pragmatic man, Stan confronted the issue with logic. He was not the villain. He'd seen an opportunity and taken advantage of it. The merchants and gambling establishments were happy to receive a partial payment when the likelihood of getting any funds was minimal.

One of the birds squawked, and Ophelia lifted the cloth. "Shh, Viola. It cannot be long now," she assured the disgruntled bird.

"In truth, Ophelia, we've been on Kenclere Hall lands for the past twenty minutes."

"We have?" She perked up at that. After recovering the birds, she leaned forward and peered out the window. "Is that your stables?"

Stan bent at the waist to look where she pointed. "It is. One of them, that is."

"You have more than one?" Ophelia sent him a

side-eyed look before resuming her scrutiny.

"I do. I also dabble in horse breeding, but not to the extent your friend Miss Slater or the Duke of Waycross do. Mine is a hobby rather than a profession."

"May I…" She cast him another brief glance. "That is, if it is not too much trouble, might I have a horse of my own?"

Aye, I'd give you the moon and stars if you asked for them.

Taken aback at his poetic thoughts, Stan nodded. But she'd turned her head away once more, so he said, "Of course. If we cannot find you a suitable mount in my stables, then we'll purchase you one."

"Oh, that's not necessary." She settled back onto the comfortable gold velvet seat. "I'm sure one of your mounts will suit."

"I meant to tell you sooner, but it slipped my mind. I've arranged with Pennington for your dowry to be put in a bank account in your name. It is yours to do with as you wish."

Mouth slack, she swung her gaze to his. "You did? Why?"

"I didn't need any incentive to marry you, Ophelia. I married you because I wanted to." Arms folded, Stan regarded her. "And I believe women aren't chattel to their husbands. They should have money to invest in whatever projects or investments are of interest to them."

"That's quite radical of you," she murmured.

"Have you anything that intrigues you?" he asked, eager to know more about the woman he'd made his wife.

"Actually," she admitted cautiously. "I've always wanted to sponsor a home for unwed mothers from all stations. Teach them a trade and provide for their essential needs."

"Very admirable and certainly much needed," Stan said. "I'll match whatever you contribute financially."

Ophelia blinked owlishly at him.

"I'm not quite the ogre I'm made out to be, Ophelia."

That put a bit of starch in her spine. She stiffened and jutted her chin out. "I never thought you were."

"Then I thank you," Stan said.

"Ogre indeed," she muttered beneath her breath.

Unlike most women of his station, Ophelia didn't appear to care for wealth, position, or possessions. And because of that, it made Stan want to shower her with gifts. To see her hazel eyes alight with surprise and her luscious mouth curve into a smile.

His focus dropped to her lips. They'd eaten fresh raspberries with their lunch when they'd changed the team of horses at Ye Old Blue Boar Inn. Her lips retained a trace of the berries' redness.

"I want to kiss you, Ophelia." Stan wouldn't impose himself on her. He'd given his word. In fact, instead of kissing her as was customary after they exchanged their vows, he'd raised her hand and pressed his mouth to her knuckles instead.

"I..." She pinkened delightfully but held his gaze. "I'd like you to kiss me, Stanford."

11

Before Ophelia could utter a shocked squeak in protest, Stanford scooped her from her seat and placed her on his lap. He waggled his raven eyebrows playfully.

"I don't need a second invitation, madam."

"You, sir, are an opportunist," Ophelia scolded, but the breathless quality of her voice belied any real censure. This impetuous Stanford had her at sixes and sevens.

She had thought she knew him, but her head and heart were at cross purposes. Her head kept warning her to tread with extreme caution, but her heart? Well, the silly, gullible organ fluttered like an inebriated moth when he directed his full charm toward her.

"When it comes to kissing my wife, I am." Stanford lowered his head until his mouth was a mere inch from hers. "Are you sure, love?"

Ophelia searched his dark blue eyes. He was so close that she could see the purple ring around his irises and the silver flecks there too. Caught up in some unnameable emotion, or perhaps it was a sensation, she managed a partial nod. More of a dip of her chin because she couldn't wrest her gaze from his.

"I am most delighted," he whispered before claiming her mouth.

In point of fact, Ophelia was rather delighted as well.

She melted into his chest, reaching one hand up to clutch at his coat lapel lest she slide onto the floor. For surely every bone in her body had turned to melted butter. She sighed, opening her mouth to the gentle prodding of Stanford's tongue.

With utter reverence, he cupped her face with one ungloved hand, cradling it as if she were the most cherished of possessions. His tongue met hers, and she gasped in shock. It wasn't an unpleasant sensation, just different.

Her blood hummed in her veins, a melody of want and need and curiosity. Her head spun with the headiness of his kiss—with the scandalous exhilaration of kissing him in a coach.

Stanford angled her against him, one steely arm supporting her as he explored the curve of her hip and then ever higher with his other hand. Lost in dizzying sensation, Ophelia arched into him, needing, wanting something more.

Something growing within her and in intensity.

When his fingers skimmed her breast—*accidentally? On purpose? Does it matter?*—Ophelia gave a throaty moan.

The sound was animalistic and ought to have appalled her. Her behavior ought to have as well. But nothing about what she and Stanford were doing disgusted her. If physical intimacy was anything like this, she mightn't want to wait a month to consummate their union.

The coach lurched, and both birds gave frightened chirps.

Stanford lifted his head, then cocked it to one side.

"I believe we have arrived at Kenclere Hall, Duchess."

Duchess. I'm a duchess now.

It would be some time before Ophelia would become accustomed to anyone calling her that.

Stanford's eyes crinkled slightly at the corners as he stared into hers. She could get lost in the depths of his beautiful eyes. Could become accustomed to his kisses and hands upon her person.

Why people called him cold and unfeeling, she couldn't imagine.

Her new husband was kind and gentle. Considerate too.

Ophelia realized with a start that she *liked* Stanford.

Truly liked him. Esteemed him as well.

When had *that* happened?

Just a week ago, she'd believed him to be a horned devil with cloven feet and a forked tail.

"Should we shock my most proper staff and have the coachman drive on a little longer so that we may indulge in more kissing?" He veered a rapid, irony-filled glance toward the coach door. "I fear the door will be opened at any moment."

"What?"

Good Lord, no.

What would his servants think of their new mistress?

That he'd married a wanton hussy? A woman with no notion of propriety or decorum?

Her passion dissipated with commendable alacrity.

Ophelia struggled to sit upright.

"You are very, *very* bad, Stanford. I must make a good first impression."

"You will, love. I have no doubt." Chuckling, he helped her into a sitting position.

She scampered to her seat, her cheeks hot with chagrin.

"Your earbob is lopsided." He pointed to her right ear. "And the top button of your spencer has come undone."

At once, she righted the jet earring and refastened the black satin button.

"You make me forget myself," she grumbled beneath her breath.

Yes, forget herself in a way that was at once alarming and thrilling.

Grinning widely, he sat back and crossed his arms. "I do?"

She glanced up from smoothing her skirts. Eyes narrowed, she pressed her lips into a contemplative line. "I see I shall have to be diligent to not compliment you too often. It goes straight to your head."

The door opened before Stanford could respond, and with a sassy I-had-the-last-word smile, she turned her attention to the ivory and emerald liveried footman—a handsome man in his mid-twenties with a scar lashing one side of his face.

He executed a perfect bow. "Welcome, Your Graces."

Naturally, Stanford had sent word ahead that they were coming. She was the only one to be taken entirely off guard when he'd announced following the wedding this morning that they weren't staying in London but would depart for Kenclere Hall after breakfast.

He'd sent a note round to the Pennington's housekeeper asking that Ophelia's possessions be packed and sent on ahead to Kenclere Hall to be unpacked before she arrived.

Stanford leaped down without using the box provided to step down. Eyes shining, he surveyed his twenty-plus servants, neatly lined up on either side of the stairs leading to a double entry door.

An elaborate door that led to—Ophelia's eyes grew wide—*a castle*. Complete with turrets and battlements. Surely there were at least three hundred rooms.

What? No moat? Drawbridge?

The forest along the long drive had obstructed the view. She'd expected an impressive manor house.

A bloody castle.

She was to be mistress of a castle?

Panic flooded Ophelia. She'd been so worried about becoming Stanford's wife that she'd not considered everything her new position entailed.

God help her. Was she up to this?

It was far, far too late now if she wasn't.

Yes, yes, she *could* do this.

It might take some time to learn everything, but Ophelia was never one to avoid a challenge. She *was* duchess material. What was more, she was going to prove it to herself, the *ton*, and to Stanford. She would show the gossipmongers and that nasty Candace Metcalfe.

Stanford held his hand out, and, more self-conscious than she could ever recall feeling, Ophelia slipped her hand in his. Welcoming the strength of his grip, she permitted him to help her from the coach.

As she alit, she asked the footman. "Could you please bring my birds?"

"Of course, Your Grace."

Grinning like a cheeky schoolboy, Stanford faced his staff. "May I present your new mistress, my wife, Ophelia, the Duchess of Asherford?"

A polite smattering of applause and broad smiles met her as the staff acknowledged their master's new wife.

Well, at least they were a friendly lot.

Ophelia glanced upward, meeting Stanford's confident gaze.

He bent his head and whispered in her ear, "Nervous, love?"

She swallowed and nodded. "I confess, I am a bit."

"I'm here. You needn't fear anything." Drawing Ophelia closer, he tucked her hand into the crook of his elbow and led her toward her new home.

To a new life. A life and a future with him.

Her tummy fluttered in giddy anticipation.

The truth slammed into Ophelia with such force that she stumbled.

At once, he steadied her. "All right?"

Incapable of speech because of the epiphany that nearly knocked her over, she somehow fashioned a smile and managed a jerky nod.

Heaven and all of the divine creatures abiding there.

Ophelia didn't just like Stanford. Indeed, she might very well be falling in love with him.

12

Kenclere Hall Rose Gardens

A fortnight later

Early morning

Whistling beneath his breath, Stan wandered the fragrant rose garden. Their petals still damp with dew, the roses he selected were only the most perfect for his sleeping wife. While Ophelia wasn't a late riser, neither was she awake, dressed, and prowling the house by six most mornings as was his wont.

Another habit formed early on when there was too much for a young man to do and not enough time or money to see it done. Even after he'd accumulated wealth and the driving need to prove himself competent no longer existed, dawn beckoned to him.

Stan wouldn't break his fast until Ophelia came down to the breakfast room at eight. To do so would deprive him of her company, which he was increasingly loath to do. To occupy himself, he'd taken to devising methods to woo her during this tranquil time he had alone.

Grinning, he snipped a coral-colored bud, then raised his head to locate the rook cawing a raucous greeting. The bird disappeared into the woodlands just as a rooster crowed. Kenclere Hall had never felt like home until Ophelia illuminated the castle with her spirit and kindness.

Every day, Stan increasingly realized what a treasure he'd been gifted in her as his wife. And every day, he became determined to win her heart. For his heart was already hers to do with as she pleased.

Of course, she didn't know that yet.

Stan had never considered himself a coward. Nonetheless, confessing his love for Ophelia and not having it reciprocated would eviscerate him. So he kept the knowledge to himself and showed her how much she meant to him in a myriad of little ways.

Fresh cut flowers. A jewel here and there. Asking Cook to prepare Ophelia's favorite foods, having received a list of them from the Duchess of Pennington.

Yes, Stan had believed he and Ophelia would suit for practical reasons. But he'd never expected to crave her company, enjoy her wit and intelligence, or find pleasure in pleasing her.

He clipped another blossom, taking a moment to smell the rose before gently placing it in the basket hanging from his bent arm. He could, of course, have assigned the task to one of his gardeners, but there was something satisfying about giving her a bouquet he'd taken the time to pick.

A wry smile twisting his mouth, Stan shook his head.

He was fast becoming a romantic sot.

The past two weeks had been the most peaceful, fulfilling, and contented of his life. No threatening letters had followed him to Kenclere Hall. Perhaps whoever the disgruntled bounder was who'd sent them had given up the game. Or perchance, the Bow Street

Runner had apprehended the villain, and Stan hadn't received word yet.

His stomach growled.

Searching the castle's windows, Stan permitted his gaze to linger on her bedchamber window. Was she awake yet?

He and Ophelia always broke their fast together. Then he'd show her more of the castle or the lands. She was particularly fond of the library, a solar in one of the turrets, and the orangery situated at the castle's rear several feet from this very rose garden.

Today, after he gave her the fragrant roses and they'd eaten, Stan intended to present the new mare to her. He'd been torn whether to let Ophelia select her own mount or to surprise her. The choice had been taken from him when he'd received notice that as partial payment for an outstanding debt, the creamy mare had been delivered to Stan's stables.

The horse was utterly perfect for Ophelia. Not too small, but not too many hands tall either. Young, but not overly so. Gentle and intelligent, Opal also had a mischievous bend. When he'd learned her name was

Opal, the decision had been made for him.

Examining the overflowing basket, he laid the clippers atop the stems and turned toward the house. He came up short upon seeing a fully clothed Ophelia standing in the doorframe of the orangery. Casting an eye to the sun, he scrunched his forehead.

It couldn't be seven yet.

Why was she downstairs so early?

"Stanford. Stanford. Come quickly." Practically bouncing on her toes, she gestured for him to hurry.

Picking up his pace, he rushed toward her, unmindful of the dew dampening his boots. As he approached, he called, "Is something amiss, Ophelia?"

"Oh, no." She gave him a radiant smile and shook her head.

His stomach toppled, and his heart tripped over itself at the sheer delight etching her beautiful face and dancing in her eyes. She wore a gown he'd never seen on her before. Of palest peach and edged in ecru lace, she looked like a flower herself. Or a piece of the forbidden fruit he yearned to taste.

When he stood before her, he extended the basket.

"I brought you flowers, darling."

"Again? You spoil me, Stanford." She gingerly lifted a rose, taking care to avoid the thorns on the stem. Eyes locked with his, she put it to her nose and inhaled. "I love the smell of roses."

He knew that.

That was why there were fresh bouquets in the house every day.

"I know you do."

Her hazel eyes grew soft. "Thank you."

Ophelia flummoxed him by standing on her toes and pressing her velvet, soft mouth to his.

He automatically reached to encircle her, to deepen the kiss, except the damnable basket was wedged between them.

She giggled and stepped away. Holding out her hand for Stan's, she wiggled her fingers. "I want to show you something amazing."

Waggling his eyebrows, he took her proffered hand. "How can I say no?"

"You cannot." Ophelia grinned.

It was true.

Not only had she thoroughly ensnared him—The Dangerous Duke—*the former dangerous duke*—but also relished it. He certainly didn't deserve this happiness. Regardless, he'd seize the joy with a vengeance and revel in every second as well.

As they approached the birds' cage, Ophelia put a finger to her lips. "Shh. They're quite nervous. I knew something was amiss a few days ago. They'd been behaving most peculiarly. But today was the first time they let me see."

"Do you always visit the orangery in the morning?" he asked.

She glanced behind her. "Not every day. Just the days I awaken early, and it's too soon to breakfast with you."

With you.

Rather than take a tray in her chamber or eat before he joined her, she also waited for him. There wasn't much of his heart that hadn't already plopped at her delicate feet, but a piece landed there just the same.

This woman was beyond remarkable.

Motioning to a nearby table, topped with potted red

and pink begonias, Ophelia said, "Put the flowers there."

Stan did so, then quirked a brow. "What is this about?"

She only smiled and led him into the cage. Moving slowly and with care, she unfastened the walk-in enclosure. She entered, and he followed, taking care to secure the latch once more.

"Look," she whispered, pointing to a straw nest the lovebirds had created.

"Well, I'll be pickled," he said, bending over to get a better look.

Viola had laid five brown-speckled ivory eggs. Orsino hovered near his mate, grazing his beak over her head.

"They are going to be parents." A brilliant smile wreathed Ophelia's face, and she sounded every bit the proud grandparent.

Wrapping an arm around her slender waist, Stan kissed the top of her head. As always, her essence engulfed him.

"Are we?" he asked.

The words were out of his mouth before he realized it.

"Are we what?" Cocking her head, Ophelia furrowed her brow.

Stan mentally shrugged.

In for a penny, in for a pound.

He'd quickly learn if he'd pressed Ophelia too hard too soon.

"Going to be parents, love?"

She faced him, tilting her neck until their eyes met. "I'd like to someday. I've always wanted several children." Her focus veered to the nest. "Five, in truth."

"Five?" Stan had never thought beyond his heir and one or two spares.

"Yes. Three boys and two girls. Naturally, I adored having a twin sister, but I always thought it would've been wonderful to have more brothers and sisters."

Truth be told, Stan had wanted brothers and sisters as well. He'd hoped his father would marry and have more children. Before he inherited the duchy and there was no more time to be a child and indulge in childish fantasies.

Stan brushed a finger along Ophelia's jaw, not missing the way her irises dilated at his touch. "That, my dear, will take some time. Don't you think?"

"Indeed. Years, I suspect." Ophelia's focus dropped to his mouth for a fraction.

His lovely, reluctant wife mightn't be quite so reluctant anymore, it seemed.

Stan lifted her chin with his bent forefinger. "Well, shouldn't we be about it then?"

Before she could respond, he claimed her mouth in a kiss meant to convey everything in his heart.

Sighing, Ophelia arched against him and twined her arms about his neck. As Viola and Orsino chirped and cooed like the proud parents to be that they were, time ceased to exist.

Stan lost track of how long he kissed Ophelia. Their breathing became one, their tongues tangling and mating. A conflagration ignited within him, soon burgeoning into an inferno he was on the cusp of losing control of.

Slowly, reluctantly, he drew away. Brushing a strand of silky golden-brown hair off of her creamy, flushed cheek, he murmured, "The first time I make love to you shall not be in a birdcage."

Ophelia burst into laughter. "I should hope not. Viola and Orsino would be quite traumatized. I believe I would as well. That floor does not look comfortable."

No, but my bed is.

Mayhap Stanford wouldn't have to wait another two weeks to introduce Ophelia to passion. To claim her as his before God and man and for all time.

She didn't pretend false modesty or shyness about the passionate exchange that had just taken place. Instead, still chuckling, she slid the latch open and stepped out.

"Ophelia?"

She glanced over her shoulder. "Yes?"

As Stan came through the door, he said, "You are a wonder." He took her hand and kissed her knuckles. "I'm so glad you are my duchess."

"I am glad too, Stanford." Her hazel eyes twinkled with suppressed mirth. "However, you still have two more weeks before I shall come to your bed."

13

Kenclere Hall Stables

15 July 1810

Four days later

"Yes, I brought you a treat. I know you expect one every day now, spoiled miss."

Ophelia extended the carrot to Opal, who gingerly took the vegetable between her strong teeth and chomped happily. Ophelia had fallen in love with the gentle blue-eyed mare the instant Stanford had led her from the stables.

The mare, named for her unusual eyes, had taken to Ophelia at once as well.

Now, Ophelia and Stanford's morning routine

included a relaxing ride before breaking their fasts. There was nothing quite as lovely and refreshing as the English countryside as a new day began. Bird calls filled the air, hares darted across the verdant meadow sprinkled with blue, pink, and yellow wildflowers, and an occasional roe deer watched them cautiously from a distance.

Today, Stanford had promised to show her the previous castle's ruins.

Several laborers toiled about the stables and immaculate grounds. All were impeccably polite and deferential.

Honestly, Ophelia had been surprised at the number of men Stanford employed. She supposed it was necessary for an estate this size, however. Particularly since not only did he grow barley, he bred and raised horses.

As he helped her onto the sidesaddle, she said, "You say the current castle was constructed over the course of fifty years in the thirteenth century, but the original castle dates from the ninth century?"

"Indeed. My ancestors were a rough lot. The first

castle was a gift for my many times' great grandfather's loyalty to William the Conqueror. There are whispers of Vikings, mercenaries, and other less savory sorts amongst my lineage." He raised his eyebrows. "Hence my moniker, the Dangerous Duke, is rather apt."

"Balderdash," Ophelia scoffed at once. She hated when he referred to himself by that unflattering name. He might be somber, stoic, and, at times, intimidating, but he was not a dangerous man. "You are no more a threat than that tiny kitten the maids are feeding in the kitchen is."

"Even kittens have claws, my dear." Stanford winked rakishly, and her pulse did that silly, wobbly thing it did too often of late.

Though she'd given her heart to her husband weeks ago, Ophelia wasn't yet prepared to admit that vulnerability. Cowardice wasn't her nature, but something held her back. She wanted to keep that secret locked inside where it was safe and protected. Something that special ought to be cherished, and given her husband's austere character, she didn't think he'd welcome the confession.

Stanford had made it abundantly clear theirs was a marriage of convenience.

Besides, it was too soon for such admissions.

After seeing her settled upon Opal, Stanford mounted his horse with masculine grace and agility that Ophelia couldn't help but appreciate. His buff-clad muscular thighs flexed and bunched as Baldric, his gelding, pranced about for a moment.

With a laugh of sheer pleasure, Ophelia reigned Opal toward the road. She hadn't expected to be so happy as Stanford's wife. Nudging the mare's side, she laughed again when the horse broke into a canter.

Stanford's laughter echoed behind her. "Baldric, they think to outrun us. Come on, old chap. That won't do at all."

In a flash, her husband raced past her. He stopped at the crest of the hill where they generally entered the meadow. Angling back to watch her, he grinned like a naughty lad.

He was happy too.

Ophelia's heart filled to bursting.

She had made him happy.

"Stanford, I've been thinking," she said as she caught up with him. "Might we have a gathering at Kenclere Hall so that I may meet the locals? I'm sure by now they've heard you're in residence with your new wife. I do not wish them to think me unfriendly or a snob."

A shadow flitted across his face before a wry smile chased it away. "Tired of me already?"

Did he really think that?

That she wanted the company of others over him?

What a pea goose.

True, Ophelia missed feminine companionship and her sister. However, every moment spent with Stanford of late was a delight.

"Don't be a baconbrain. I enjoy your company very much." She looked toward the meadow and the grass swaying ever so slightly in the light breeze. The industrious hum of bees going about their business filled the air. "I merely want to make a good impression among your friends."

"I appreciate your conscientiousness, Ophelia, and I promise we will entertain soon." He gave her one of his smoldering looks. "Can you blame me for wanting you all to myself for a little while longer?"

A flush of pleasure stole over her.

When he looked at her like that, all of her remaining common sense took to wing. She would be wise not to dwell on where her thoughts directed her when that happened. They were not the least chaste.

"Just let me know when the time is appropriate," she said, steering Opal around a divot in the ground. "I shall need help with the guest list."

Stanford nodded rather distractedly as he skimmed his keen gaze this way and that. The dark blue of his hunting jacket deepened his eye color to cobalt. Daily, she came to appreciate how handsome he was—not in the pretty, affected way of so many peers. But rather, he was attractive in a rugged, manly manner that very much appealed to her.

For the first time this morning, Ophelia noticed the tense lines bracketing his mouth and the stiffness of his shoulders and spine. His expression had become pinched, especially between his eyebrows.

Something was amiss.

Catching her lower lip between her teeth, Ophelia pondered. Should she ask him about whatever troubled him or pretend ignorance? If Stanford wanted her to know, wouldn't he have mentioned it?

Some things a person preferred to keep to themselves. Mayhap she could take his mind off of whatever bothered him.

"The castle isn't along our normal route, I presume." She could've kicked herself for the idiocy of her remark. Of course, it wasn't. If it had been, he would've shown it to her before this.

"No. We ride a half-mile along this lane and then take an overgrown track to the site." He half-turned and looked behind them. "I wonder if I oughtn't to have had a groom or two come along as well."

"But why?" She treasured these private times with him. They inevitably resulted in a few passionate kisses and caresses.

Ophelia had discovered she quite liked both. And both made her eager to sample the marriage bed. Nonetheless, she still hesitated to fully become Stanford's in every way. Once she did, she feared the

Ophelia she now was would cease to be.

It was silly and illogical, but the dread was genuine.

"It's been some time since I've been there," Stanford said, drawing her back to the present. "The path may be more difficult to pass through than I've anticipated, and an extra hand or two would've been welcome to clear the way."

She lifted one shoulder and adjusted her grip on the reins. "Well, if it is impassable for the horses, we can either go on foot or ask to have the path cleared, and we can visit another day."

He gave her a sideways glance. "Are you always so pragmatic, my darling Ophelia?"

Not always.

Not when it came to her husband.

Most especially not when he called her his darling.

Before them, a swallow dove after an insect, then gracefully swooped high into the air again. She and Stanford rode on abreast of one another, and the silence between them was not quite contentment.

It was because she couldn't stop wondering what had him distracted and uneasy.

Suddenly, several crows took flight from the woodlands, their coarse caws breaking the summer day's lazy serenity. Simultaneously, the warning cries of squirrels filled the air.

Stanford's black eyebrows lashed together as he peered intently into the moving shadows within the woodlands to their left.

"Ophelia," he said beneath his breath in a tone that raised her nape hairs. "Turn Opal around and run back to the stables. *Now.*"

She opened her mouth to ask why when a movement caught her eye, and a frisson of fear skittered along her spine and clawed at her stomach.

Someone was in the woods.

Someone dangerous from Stanford's reaction.

"Stanford?" Her voice trembled the merest bit. "What—?"

"Now, Ophelia! Go!"

In a blink, he brought Baldric around and kicked the horse's sides. The gelding lurched forward at the exact moment Opal did.

"No matter what, Ophelia." Stanford's words came

harsh and choppy. "Do not stop. You must get to the stables. My men will know what to do."

A shot rang out, cracking through the air like a blast of thunder.

"Goddammit," Stanford roared, looking behind them. "Ride, Ophelia, ride."

Ophelia wasn't a talented rider. In truth, she'd only taken up riding after Sophronie had volunteered to give her and a few others riding lessons. At this pounding pace, she struggled to keep her seat and control Opal.

Jaw set, she focused on the stables.

Searing pain lanced her back before she heard the report of the second gunshot.

"I think…Stanford."

She swallowed against the agony burning in her back.

"I've been shot," she mumbled as a buzzing began in her ears and misty gray obscured the edges of her vision.

In the distance, men ran toward them, shouting. A few stable hands charged forward on horses too.

"Oh, God," Stanford half groaned, half-shouted.

"No. No. Please, God. No."

Would the crazed gunman try to shoot Stanford too?

As Ophelia tipped to the side, she let the reins slip from her fingers.

She was going to fall.

The stables were too far away.

I'm sorry, Stanford.

Stanford was there, catching her in his strong arms and pulling her onto his lap.

A scream tore from Ophelia's throat as unimaginable pain nearly made her swoon. Or wretch. Or both.

"Forgive me, my love." Hunched over as if to protect her, he cradled her to his chest.

Forgive him? Why?

"I did this to you, my dearest love. This is my fault." Stanford's voice cracked on the last words.

Why was he talking such gibberish?

Of course, it wasn't his fault.

It was so hard to keep her eyelids open. The buzzing had increased to a thunderous roar, and only a pinprick of light was visible, though her eyes were open.

"Stanford?" she managed weakly.

"Shh," he murmured in the tremulous tenor of a tortured man. "Save your strength."

"I must tell you…" Ophelia's words slurred together.

Talking had become difficult too.

Sweet oblivion beckoned her. The pain would cease if she let the darkness claim her.

Was this what it was like to die?

"Stan…ford," she whispered again, the effort monumental.

"Don't die, Ophelia. I forbid it. Do you hear me? Do not die, my love."

Something warm and wet landed on her cheek.

Squinting, she peered up at his dear face. A hazy fuzziness obstructed her view.

Another droplet hit her cheek, and then another.

Why, he was weeping.

The strongest, toughest man she'd ever known was crying because he was afraid she was going to die.

In truth, she feared as much as well. And she'd

never told Stanford that she loved him.

It wasn't too late. It wasn't.

Ophelia could still tell him.

Now.

She must tell him.

Blackness whirled around her mind. She allowed her eyelashes to flutter closed.

"I…love…you."

His animalistic cry was the last thing she comprehended before slipping into insensibility.

14

Kenclere Hall

Duchess's bedchamber

17 July 1810

Nearly midnight

S tan awoke with a start, icy fear tunneling through his veins.

Blast and damn.

He'd fallen asleep. Keeping a vigil at Ophelia's bedside, he'd not slept since she'd been shot, and his exhaustion had simply overtaken him.

He'd dreamed that she was slumped in his arms again, her blood soaking his trousers. He'd been chanting, "I love you. I love you. I love you."

Would he ever have the chance to say those words to her and see her reaction?

The fire burned low in the hearth. Stan would need to stoke it soon, though no chill penetrated the bedchamber this July evening. On the bedside tables, only nubs remained of the tapers that had flickered happily a few hours ago.

Awash in a cold sweat and with dread choking him, he lifted his head from the ivory and lavender coverlet his insensate wife lay beneath. Nerves strung tight enough to snap, he stared at her chest, willing it to rise and fall as he'd done these past two interminable days.

Her face as pale as the prim white nightgown buttoned to her neck, Ophelia continued to breathe.

"Thank you, God," Stan whispered, lifting her hand and then placing a tender kiss on her cool palm.

Cool palm?

Exhilaration engulfed him, and the relief was so heady that dizziness overcame him for a moment.

Had Ophelia's fever finally broken?

Yes, yes! Stan could see that now in the weak firelight. Sweat no longer beaded her face or saturated her night rail.

"Please get better, my love. I want to tell you I love you too. I want to spend the rest of my life showing you how much I adore you." Stan pressed his mouth to Ophelia's hand again before threading his fingers through hers.

He hadn't left her side except to use the necessary. In truth, even then, he was afraid she'd die while he was away. The way Filson had eyed him this morning, and his valet, Pringlehurst's, nose had twitched this afternoon, suggested Stan was very much in need of a bath.

To satisfy his servants' offended sensibilities, Stan had stripped, washed with the cold water in the basin in his chamber, and then donned clean clothing—all in under five minutes. After cleansing his teeth and declining a shave, much to Pringlehurst's chagrin, he'd returned to Ophelia's chamber.

Stan wasn't leaving his wife again until she woke up, and he knew beyond a doubt that she would recover.

Doctor Plack said Ophelia had either been incredibly lucky, or the Almighty had protected her. The ball hadn't struck any major organs.

After the physician had removed the lead, he'd announced with a somber nod of his bald head, "The duchess lost a great deal of blood, Your Grace. Still, the greatest risk for her now is infection."

"She must survive, Doctor Plack." Stan had heard the desperation in his voice, yet hang his pride. Pride didn't giggle and smile. Pride didn't get excited over a pair of lovebirds laying eggs. Pride didn't make him eager to get out of bed in the morning. Pride hadn't turned him from an unsmiling curmudgeon into a lovesick fool.

As the doctor snapped his well-used leather bag shut, he said, "I shall call every morning and evening to monitor her progress and change her bandage. Let her sleep. It's the body's way of healing itself. If you can persuade her to accept either, I recommend strong chicken stock and water. Naturally, I left laudanum for her pain as well."

Once he'd taken himself off and Stanford had cleared the fussing maids from the room, he'd pulled a chair beside Ophelia's bed. She was lying at death's door because of him. Because he'd used a controversial means to initially fill the duchy's coffers.

Never mind that he'd given up acquiring the debts of others years ago, although several men still owed him considerable sums. Prudent investments of those tainted funds had further deepened the dukedom's reserves. Still, he'd do it over again. A lad of fourteen had few resources available to him, and sheer ingenuity had motivated Stan.

However, he should've been more compassionate. Should've shown grace and mercy where appropriate instead of lumping all of the insolvents into one offensive pile deserving of his scorn.

Now the most precious of women, the person he cared most about in this world and the one to come perhaps as well, might be taken from him.

No. No. By damn.

Stanford could not—would not—countenance it.

Ophelia *would* get well.

He'd talked to her these past days. Telling her things he'd never revealed to another. Encouraging her to wake up and suggesting alphabetical names for their five children.

Anastasia and Aleric. Bernadette and Bentley. Chesney and Chandler. Delphine and Demetrius. Estelle and Emerson.

How he wanted to see her grow heavy with his children. To raise them together.

"Wake up, my love. Please wake up. I swear you'll not regret marrying me. I'll see you happy. I vow it with my life, my precious darling."

Ophelia lay corpse-like, waxen and beautiful, her hair plaited in a long rope. If only she'd move. Her lashes flutter. Moan in her sleep. Something. *Anything.*

The crazed fiend who'd shot her hadn't escaped the well-trained runners. Only the culprit hadn't been one of the men whose debts he'd collected but Colton DeBroux, the fourteen-year-old son of an aristocrat. He'd seen his mother take his sisters and leave his drunkard father and him behind. A father who raved incessantly about The Duke of Asherford as the man who'd ruined him.

And then Colton DeBroux's inebriated father had been set upon by thieves as he stumbled home late one night. He'd not recovered, leaving DeBroux and his sisters fatherless.

The boy was the same age Stan had been when he'd been forced to take on a man's responsibilities. After meeting with Colton DeBroux and determining that he was a decent lad whose fear and anger had led him astray, Stan hadn't pressed charges against him.

Instead, Stan had directed his man of affairs to arrange for the boy to go to school. He'd also sent monies to Colton's mother, along with a letter asking her to return to her son. She had done so, and the family had been reunited.

Shoulders hunched, his wife's delicate hand resting between his own, Stan prayed. He wasn't a particularly religious man, but if there was a God and he heard and answered prayers, Stan would pray.

Ophelia stirred, and he jerked his head up.

"Ophelia?"

Her eyelashes trembled, and a soft moan passed her lips.

"Darling. You're safe. You're at Kenclere Hall in your bed."

Once more, her eyelashes fluttered, and slowly, agonizingly slowly, she opened her eyes.

Hot tears stung behind Stan's eyelids, but he blinked them away and gave her a tender smile. "Hello, darling."

Brow puckered, she gazed at him. "I was shot?"

"Yes, sweetheart. Dr. Plack removed the lead ball, and you've slept for over two days."

She was awake.

My love is awake, his soul sang over and over.

"Why?"

"Why were you shot?" Stan cupped her soft cheek. "We'll talk about that later. Are you hungry?"

She thought about that for a moment, then gave a slight nod. "I think I am ravenous."

"Excellent."

He rose and rang the bell. Almost instantly, a scratching sounded at the chamber door. Stan opened the door a couple of inches and asked for a tray to be sent up.

"Her Grace has awoken."

"Praise be!" exclaimed the housemaid, grinning so

widely that her chin nearly disappeared into her dimpled cheeks. "I'll be back with everything you asked for before two shakes of a lamb's tail, Your Grace."

Returning to Ophelia's bedside, Stan asked, "Are you in pain?"

She nodded. "It feels like a hot blade was jammed into my back. It burns and aches."

Not too far from the truth there.

"I'm so glad you are awake, my love. You scared ten years off my life." He eyed the mattress. There was plenty of room for him to sit beside her, but Stan didn't want to jostle Ophelia.

"Come." She patted the bed. "I would have you lie beside me."

Tentatively, taking care not to bump her or move the mattress unnecessarily, he lay down beside her. He propped his head on one elbow.

"I was so afraid I would lose you, Ophelia."

"You look tired." She grazed her fingertips across his bristly jaw. "And you need a shave."

"I couldn't leave you." Stan clasped her hand and kissed her exploring fingers.

"I think I knew you were here," she murmured. "I felt your presence."

Gazing into her eyes, he saw her love reflected for him there. How this remarkable woman could love him, he couldn't comprehend. Brushing a kiss on her cheek, he trailed his knuckles along her jaw. "I love you, Ophelia."

Such joy lit her hazel eyes that his heart seemed as if it might explode from his chest.

"I didn't know." Eyes wide with wonder, she said, "I would've told you that I loved you sooner, but I was afraid you didn't feel the same way."

"I think I've loved you from the first moment I saw you, my darling. My heart knew you were the one for me, and I botched the whole thing by declaring we would suit. That was about as romantic as a swim in the Thames in winter." Stan kissed her mouth. "But I knew I loved you when you told me I couldn't always have my own way."

"*That* made you fall in love with me?" Ophelia scrunched her nose. "I wasn't at my best that night."

"Neither was I."

She lay a hand on his chest, right above where his heart pulsed a robust and steady rhythm. "I do love you, Stanford. I didn't expect to." Ophelia glanced away for a moment then returned her attention to him. "But I do, and I don't want to wait to consummate our vows any longer. I want to have your child."

Yes, the human heart could burst from happiness.

"I was naming our children while you slept," he said. "Alphabetical names, in point of fact."

"Alphabetical?" Ophelia looked thoroughly nonplussed. "You're not serious."

"Anastasia and Aleric. Bernadette and Bentley. Chesney and Chandler. Delphine and Demetrius. Estelle and Emerson." He raised a finger each time. "You said you wanted five children."

A giggle escaped her before she clapped a hand over her mouth. "Those are...*interesting* names. Florencia and Frederick for F?"

Stan recalled that day in her sister's drawing room when they'd become officially betrothed. She'd teased him then too.

"Minx." He growled good-naturedly and nipped her shoulder.

"Can we not make love, Stan? I'm ready." A delightful blush tinted her cheeks. "I've been ready."

Stan's groin tightened at her invitation. "As much as I'd love to accept that most tantalizing invitation, my dear, we will have to wait until you are fully recovered."

"How long will that take?" A pout turned her mouth downward, and she angled her head. She was quite endearing in her sulk. "I've already waited three weeks."

Eyebrows raised, Stan said, "As long as it takes for you to fully recover. I shall take no risks with your health."

"Botheration," she muttered before giving a dramatic sigh.

"But, my wanton wife, there are other ways to find pleasure together."

Her gaze careened back to his, inquisitive and hopeful. "There are?"

"Indeed, there are." Trailing a finger along the edge of her bodice, he grinned.

"Will you show me?"

And he did. Quite satisfactorily too.

The Asherford's Restoration Home

London, England

September 1815

Ophelia could scarcely contain her excitement. If she weren't heavy with her third child, she'd have bounced upon her toes. She placed her palms on her stomach. "Will you make your brother or your sister happy, little one?"

Four-year-old Alexander insisted only a brother would do while two-year-old Bethany threw quite a tantrum when she'd been told the baby Ophelia carried might be a boy.

"No boys," Bethany declared before burying her

face in Ophelia's shoulder and bursting into tears.

Today was the day Ophelia and Stanford had worked for and anticipated for over five years. Slipping her hand into his, she said, "I can never thank you enough for helping me make this a reality, Stan."

She'd long since stopped addressing him by his full name.

"It was your dream, darling. You deserve the credit for all of it." He trailed his gaze around the prestigious crowd, many of whom had committed to becoming patrons for the home for unwed mothers. "I'm delighted for you."

"Excuse me, Your Graces. It's almost time for the ribbon cutting." Mrs. Gertrude Marlow, the home's director, beamed at them. "The good Lord is smiling down from heaven this day. Indeed, he is."

The first twenty of one hundred women the facility had been remodeled to accommodate had already taken up residence. To protect their privacy, none were present for the official opening of The Asherford's Restoration Home. Most were prostitutes whose circumstances had forced them into the profession.

Others were from workhouses or even debtors' prison. Some were domestics who'd been taken advantage of by their licentious employers. All were welcome at The Asherford Restoration Home.

Ophelia had chosen the name because here, these unfortunate women would have their pride and dignity restored. Here they stood a chance of becoming something other than an object of scorn or pity.

"Come along, darling." Stan guided her through the excited crowd until they stood before the entry door, where a bright red ribbon had been draped across the entrance. He kissed her cheek. "This is your day."

How was it possible she grew to love him more every day?

Django Bostock had done her the greatest of favors that long-ago day atop Gipsy Hill. Had he not behaved the cad and she'd been compromised, she mightn't have ever known the happiness she shared with Stan.

Clearing her throat, she waited until the buzz of anticipation had calmed.

"Thank you for joining the Duke of Asherford and myself today as we officially open the doors to The

Asherford Restoration Home. Without your generosity and commitment to supporting this worthy cause, this charitable venture would never have been possible. Please, come inside and tour the facility. You'll find an assortment of refreshments in the dining room."

Ophelia cut the crimson ribbon and then passed the scissors to a nearby gentleman. Amid a flurry of excited chatter, she swept into the home for unwed women with her husband's protective arm about her waist.

"Ophelia, you should be so proud," Rayne, the Duchess of Kincade, said as she swooped in to buss Ophelia's cheek. She'd come from Scotland for the event. "Do you remember that day in Hyde Park where we rued marriage because we wanted more out of life?"

"I do, indeed."

Rayne laughed and patted her own extended tummy. "Now we are wed to incredible men. Marriage is good, isn't it?"

"I should say so," Gabriella interrupted before giving Rayne a kiss on the cheek. "You look well, Rayne."

"I am. I miss all of you, of course, but Sophronie is

only an hour away, and Justina's Aunt Emily is less than two."

Gabriella laughed and shook her head. "I never would've believed Sophronie and Waycross would wed. I thought they despised one another."

"Sometimes, love is camouflaged as strife or dislike," Ophelia said, catching Stan's eye.

"Ladies, if you will excuse us?" he said.

Rayne and Gabriella nodded.

"Of course," they said in unison before turning into the throng.

Stan threaded her hand through the crook of his elbow. "I want to show you something."

"What?" Ophelia had planned this grand opening down to the last detail. If something were amiss, she ought to know. "Is there a problem?"

Stan looked over his shoulder as they slipped into a spotless corridor. "Not unless you consider it a problem that I wish to spend a few moments alone with my wife celebrating her accomplishment."

"Stan," Ophelia laughed. "I cannot abandon our guests."

Giving her a roguish grin, he opened a nearby door and escorted her inside. Four small windows at the top of the room filtered light into the closet.

A broom closet.

"This is your idea of romantic?" She twisted her mouth into a wry smile.

His grin grew decidedly seductive. "I distinctly recall, not so very long ago, when *you* waylaid me in the larder, my love."

Ophelia blushed furiously. "That was in our home. Our servants know to knock before they enter."

Only because one unfortunate maid hadn't announced herself before opening the library door at Kenclere Hall. After the incident, Stan had asked each of his majordomos to instruct the staff to always knock before entering a room with a door.

"Well, I want to congratulate my remarkable wife here. Now." He dipped his head and captured her mouth in a searing kiss.

Ophelia melted into him, a puppet at his command. The kiss was long and passionate, and all too soon, other feelings began to stir. Pulling away, she curved her mouth. "If I weren't so enormous, we might extend our play."

"You are never more beautiful than when you carry my child." He dropped a kiss upon her nose, then proceeded to straighten her clothing. When she passed his inspection, he cupped her face and kissed her again. "I love you."

"And I love you." Hugging him tightly, Ophelia said, "I'm glad that, in my case, you always have your way."

"I am too, because a life without you would be no life at all."

About the Author

USA Today Bestselling, award-winning author COLLETTE CAMERON® scribbles Scottish and Regency historicals featuring dashing rogues and scoundrels and the intrepid damsels who reform them. Blessed with an overactive and witty muse that won't stop whispering new romantic romps in her ear, she's lived in Oregon her entire life, though she dreams of living in Scotland part-time. A self-confessed Cadbury chocoholic, you'll always find a dash of inspiration and a pinch of humor in her sweet-to-spicy timeless romances®.

Explore **Collette's worlds** at
collettecameron.com!

Join her **VIP Reader Club** and **FREE newsletter**.
Giggles guaranteed!

FREE BOOK: Join Collette's The Regency Rose®
VIP Reader Club to get updates on book releases, cover
reveals, contests, and giveaways she reserves
exclusively for email and newsletter followers. Also,
any deals, sales, or special promotions are offered to
club members first. She will not share your name or
email, nor will she spam you.

http://bit.ly/TheRegencyRoseGift

Follow Collette on BookBub
https://www.bookbub.com/authors/collette-cameron

Thank you for reading LOVED BY A DANGEROUS DUKE. I hope you've enjoyed the latest installment in my SEDUCTIVE SCOUNDRELS SERIES. I introduced Ophelia to you several books ago and briefly mentioned Stanford in a few as well. I knew what her past was, but I hadn't yet figured out what his personal story would be—what would make him into a callous, seemingly uncaring snob. But, as you learned, Stanford had a good heart and made amends for his earlier, shall we say, unpleasantness. Personally, I enjoy stories where the hero and heroine don't know they are in love until a crisis forces them to acknowledge their affection.

It might seem terribly unjust that Ophelia was considered compromised simply because she was seen disheveled in the company of a man. Societal strictures were much different two hundred years ago. Unless married or a family member, men and women weren't even permitted to touch the opposite sex's bare hand. (Now you know why every one of higher station wore gloves!)

You may have noticed several references to Sophronie Slater and the Duke of Waycross in LOVED BY A DANGEROUS DUKE. Their story releases soon. To make sure you don't miss it, subscribe to The Regency Rose, my newsletter (Get a free book too!). I also have a fabulous VIP Reader Group on Facebook. If you're a fan of my books and historical romance, I'd love to have you join me. You'll also be the first to see new covers, read exclusive excerpts, be the first to know about contests and giveaways, help me pick titles and name characters, and much, much more!

If you'd like to learn a bit more about the other characters mentioned in LOVED BY A DANGEROUS DUKE, here are their books.

Rayne Wellbrook: THE DEBUTANTE AND THE DUKE.

Gabriella and Maxwell Pennington: ONLY A DUKE WOULD DARE.

Sophronie Slater and the Duke of Waycross: HOW TO WIN A DUKE'S HEART-the next book in the series.

Jessica, Duchess of Banbridge: WOOED BY A WICKED DUKE.

Please consider telling other readers why you enjoyed this book by reviewing it. I also truly adore hearing from my readers. You can contact me on my website and, while you are there, explore my author world. If you enjoyed reading Ophelia and Stanford's story, be sure to check out the other books in my SEDUCTIVE SCOUNDRELS SERIES.

Hugs,

Collette

A Diamond for a Duke

Seductive Scoundrels, Book One

A dour duke. A wistful wallflower.
An impossible match.

Jules, Sixth Duke of Dandridge disdains Society and all its trappings, preferring the country's solitude and peace. Already jaded after the woman he loved died years ago, he's become even more so since unexpectedly inheriting a dukedom's responsibilities and finding himself the target of every husband-hunting vixen and matchmaker mother in London.

Jemmah Dament has adored Jules from afar for years—since before her family's financial and social reversals. She dares not dream she can win a duke's heart any more than she hopes to escape the life of servitude imposed on her by an uncaring mother. Jemmah knows full well Jules is too far above her station now. Besides, his family has already selected his perfect duchess: a poised, polished, exquisite blueblood.

chance encounter reunites Jules and Jemmah, resulting in a passionate interlude neither can forget. Jules realizes he wants more—much more—than Jemmah's sweet kisses or her warming his bed. He must somehow convince her to gamble on a dour duke. But can Jemmah trust a man promised to another? One who's sworn never to love again?